Bryony

&

Roses

T. Kingfisher

Other Works

As T. Kingfisher

Nine Goblins (Goblinhome Book 1)
Toad Words & Other Stories
The Seventh Bride
Bryony & Roses
Summer in Orcus

As Ursula Vernon

From Sofawolf Press:

Black Dogs Duology
House of Diamond
Mountain of Iron

Digger Series
Digger Omnibus Edition

It Made Sense At The Time

For kids:

Dragonbreath Series
Hamster Princess Series
Castle Hangnail
Nurk: The Strange Surprising Adventures of a Somewhat Brave
Shrew

Anthologies:

Comics Squad: Recess!
Funny Girl
Best of Apex Magazine
The Long List
Peter S. Beagle's *The New Voices of Fantasy*

Bryony & Roses

by T. Kingfisher

Argyll Productions
Dallas, Texas

.

For my mom,
from whom I probably
inherited the gardening
thing

Table of Contents

CHAPTER ONE

She was going to die because of the rutabagas.

Bryony pushed her cloak back from her face and looked up. The space between Fumblefoot's ears had become her entire world for the past half-hour, and she was a little surprised at how large the forest was when she finally lifted her eyes.

Unfortunately, it was all covered in a thick blanket of snow.

Her pony continued plodding forward, the snow wet and sloughing around his hooves. Even with her teeth chattering, Bryony could appreciate the beauty of the snow—fat flakes falling in a steady, business-like manner, black tree trunks fading into soft grey, the way snow piled up on top of the evergreen branches and bore them down to the ground.

It was a pity that all that beauty was going to kill them.

The pony staggered a bit. Bryony patted his shoulder as he got his feet back underneath him. It might be a sign of exhaustion, but then again, Fumblefoot came by his name honestly, and he could just be clumsy.

Please just be clumsy, old fellow.

She wished that she could get off and lead him, but once she did that, it was only a matter of time.

She hadn't felt her feet in nearly an hour. Even if Fumblefoot somehow staggered onto the road to the village, she suspected that she'd be down a couple of toes by the time they made it home.

Farewell, little pinkie toes. I can't say I ever really appreciated you, but I suspect that I will miss you very much once you're gone.

Rutabagas. Of all the stupid things to die for.

The problem with rutabagas was that they liked a long growing season if they could get it, and the earlier you planted them the better. Bryony had no great love of rutabagas—they were basically somewhat insipid turnips, fit only for stews and roasts—but she'd also never had any great success growing them, and that was a direct affront to her gardening skills.

When her friend Elspeth in Skypepper Village had sent word that she had some particularly hardy rutabagas last year, and would be happy to share the seeds, Bryony had saddled up Fumblefoot and made the five-hour journey to Skypepper. It was a little early in the spring, sure, but you really couldn't get the seeds in the ground too quickly, and there were all sorts of ways to coax the seedlings along if it looked like it was going to frost.

Bryony's lips twisted sourly. She tucked her gloved hands under her armpits, leaving the reins looped over the saddle horn. (Fumblefoot would have landed flat on his face if he tried to bolt at the best of times. He would no more have tried to run in the snow than he would have tried to fly.)

Frost. Heh.

Freakish late season blizzard, on the other hand...

Most of her plants would probably do fine, even if her sister hadn't gotten out and covered them. Sadly, Bryony and Fumblefoot wouldn't fare nearly so well as the plants.

Fumblefoot stumbled again. The wind was beginning to pick up. Bryony watched the snowfall between the pony's ears, and saw it begin to fall slantwise. When she lifted her chin off her chest to look around, the forest seemed smaller, closed in, as if they moved through a series of snowy rooms.

Beets, now, those were useful. Beets you could do something with. Tomatoes, definitely. It went without saying that a good tomato was worth dying over—if not your *personal* death, then certainly the neighbor's, who would insist on growing a tomato the size of a baby's head and then waving a hand and saying "Oh, well, nothing to it, really, I just put 'em in the ground and give 'em a drop of water now and again."

Obviously if such a neighbor was interred in the compost heap, no jury of gardeners would ever convict you.

Corn, too. Sweet corn was a glorious thing, particularly in summer, and while Bryony would not personally have been inclined to die for it, there were stories that whole civilizations were in the habit of sacrificing people to ensure the corn harvest. And wheat was so tied in with blood that even now if you went too far up into the hills at the wrong time of year, you'd best check the scarecrows *very carefully* to make sure that one of them wasn't a former travelling salesman.

Bryony sighed. Nobody in the history of the world had ever sacrificed anybody to the rutabagas. The issue simply did not arise.

She wiggled her fingers inside her gloves, yanking them free of the fabric and folding them up against her palm to try to warm them. She mostly succeeded in making her palms colder.

Her sisters were going to miss her. Bryony felt a pang thinking of them. Holly was probably going to the window every few minutes and pushing the curtains aside to look for her. Iris was likely sitting beside the fireplace, working on her embroidery and making endless cups of tea.

At least it probably won't hurt, she thought glumly. *I hear you feel really warm right before you freeze to death.*

It was hard to get upset. She was too cold. Her eyelashes had ice on them, and if she cried it would freeze on her cheeks. It was easier simply to tuck her hands in her armpits and let her chin sink to her chest and let Fumblefoot lead them through the woods. He was probably no better at finding the road than she was—Fumblefoot was a very inferior pony, or else Bryony and her sisters would never have been able to afford him—but the world was nothing but snow now, and anything resembling landmarks had vanished under white.

She tried to summon some anguish over her impending demise, but her mind rapidly wandered to the rutabaga seeds and then to the garden, and from there death could not compete.

I'll miss the garden this spring. Damnit. I hope Holly will remember that she needs to spread manure on it—Iris won't, Iris hates the very thought of manure. And someone has to weed the bee balm back, or it'll eat the whole flowerbed, and this was the year I was really hoping that the sage would take off...

Her thoughts continued in this vein for quite some time, punctuated occasionally by rubbing her nose (which was very cold, and in the way of cold noses, dripping) until she realized that Fumblefoot had stopped walking and lifted her head.

They'd found an impossible road.

CHAPTER TWO

It wasn't the main road. The road between Skypepper and Lostfarthing was broad enough for two wagons to pass abreast. This was narrower, wide enough for two horses perhaps, and there was a stone wall running along the right hand side.

The problem was that there *wasn't* any such road in the woods between Skypepper and Lostfarthing. There wouldn't be any point to it. Cutting the woods was strictly forbidden by royal decree, and there was a certain understanding among the villagers that it was in everybody's best interest if the king never had reason to send someone around to check on the forest. Poaching here was not so much a crime as a way of life, and if foresters and game wardens showed up demanding to know where all the trees had gone, a lot of people were going to go very hungry before they went away again.

There were a lot of deer in the woods—and elk and wolves and even a few of the rare forest bison (which was why it was a royal preserve in the first place.)

What there most certainly *wasn't* was a high stone wall, inset with a pair of iron gates with twining wrought-iron roses.

Saying they didn't exist did nothing to negate the fact that Bryony was currently looking at them.

They were lovely gates. An inch of snow sat atop every metal curve, giving the iron roses substance. The stone pilings on either side of the gate rose taller than her head, and were topped with two stone horses, their rearing bodies strangely elongated by the coat of snow.

Just visible through the iron gates was the grey outline of a manor house.

Bryony sat on the pony and stared.

There could not be a manor house. There had never been a manor house anywhere near Lostfarthing. Nobles did not come to Lostfarthing. It was not possible for a noble to disgrace themselves badly enough to be exiled this far east. The Duke of Entwood had been convicted of black magic, cannibalism, *and* high treason, and while he'd been burned at the stake, his heirs had only been sent as far east as Blue Lady, which was still two day's travel *west* of Skypepper.

The questionable delights of a village of a hundred and fifty souls was not sufficient to attract aristocrats in the summer, let alone during the short but vigorous winters, when the road was often snowed closed for a week or more at a time.

Nevertheless, there were gates. Insisting that there could not be gates did not make them go away. And looming beyond them, a grey shadow on the grey sky, was a distant roofline.

"My b-brain has frozen, and I'm hallucinating," Bryony said. Fumblefoot put an ear in her direction.

The snow continued to fall thick and fast. Bryony clumsily pulled her glove back on with her teeth and slid off the pony's back. The snow came up halfway to her knees.

Perhaps it was a convent. That made more sense. There was an order of nuns in Lostfarthing, the Order of St. Agnes, and they had been there forever. This was certainly not the current convent, which was smaller and had a much-mended deer fence instead of a wall, but it was just barely possible that they had once had a bigger convent in the woods—or perhaps there had been another order of nuns or monks or other serious and celibate folk—and here it was. The king frequently granted land to religious orders out on the fringes of the kingdom, because it got them out of the capital and meant that they stopped demanding things.

"That's it," said Bryony to the pony. "It's an old abandoned convent. The gates and the wall have held up very well, and I admit I've never heard of one out here, but that's the only possible explanation." She wiped her gloved hand across her eyelashes to clear the film of ice. "It's probably in ruins, but if there are a few walls still standing, maybe we can get out of the wind long enough not to die."

She reached out a hand to push the wrought-iron roses, and the gate swung open as silently as snowfall.

"Very w-well oiled ruins," she said to Fumblefoot, who looked at her as if she were crazy.

She picked up the pony's reins and led him through the gate. When she turned back to shut the gate—to keep out what? Snow-crazed bandits?—she felt her stomach give a funny little flip and watched the gate close by itself.

"Very w-well-weighted," she said. "Yes. One of the nuns was clearly a m-m-master ironworker."

Fumblefoot put his cheek against her shoulder and gazed at her mournfully, clearly hoping that if he stared long enough, she would produce warmth and oats and perhaps a stable.

"C-c-c'mon, fella, let's get ins-s-side." She gathered up the reins and looked up at the outline of the large building. If she had been warmer, she might have been a little bit afraid, but she was going to freeze to death soon, and her teeth were chattering so loudly that it was difficult to keep her thoughts together. They seemed to rattle apart before they could get anywhere.

Not being able to feel her feet did not make walking any easier. She floundered in the snow, and Fumblefoot slipped and limped along behind her.

It was a long way to the building. She could not tell what material the pathway was made from, underneath the crunching snow, but some square objects lined the pathway, their edges barely visible under the drifted snow. More walls?

When she strayed to one side and brushed her gloved hand across one, branches poked and caught under the snow, and she caught a glimpse of green.

Her lip curled. Boxwoods. Typical. She'd never liked boxwoods even before they had moved to Lostfarthing—no fruits, barely any flowers, all the purpose they served was to be chopped and clipped into ridiculous shapes for the amusement of aristocrats.

Bryony had slipped and slid down the pathway, Fumblefoot plodding along, for a good half-minute when it occurred to her that boxwoods needed pruning (yet another reason that she was not fond of them) and unless the abandoned convent still kept a gardening staff, the neat cubical hedge would be a thicket in two seasons.

Ah. Hmm.

She glared at the drifts concealing the hedge.

Maybe they're…slow-growing boxwoods. Dwarf boxwoods. Only need pruning every hundred years. Bryony grinned sourly to herself. *Hey, let's take cuttings, we'll breed them and sell them to aristocrats in the capital for a fortune…*

No. There were few things as immutable in life as the need to prune the shrubs. Either there were people out here after all, or she'd stumbled onto…something else.

"M-might as well s-say it," she told Fumblefoot. "*M-m-magic.*" Fumblefoot snorted.

Keeping a boxwood hedge trimmed was a pretty wasteful use of magic, in Bryony's opinion, but then so much magic seemed to be frivolous. If wizards could invent a charm to keep the deer out of the garden, now, or to age compost overnight—now *that* would be something useful. But no, if you were a wizard, you were far too important to fool about with that sort of thing, and would be charging money for expensive frivolities, like making sure your carriage horses had matching coats, or that your silk dress rippled with embroidery that changed color to match your surroundings.

Actually, compared to that, a permanently trimmed hedge seemed almost practical.

I don't have any proof. Maybe there's people here. Probably there's people here. After all, what's more likely—that there's a hidden manor house between home and Skypepper, or that somebody left magical self-trimming boxwoods lying around?

The snowy roadway ended in a circular carriageway, with an enormous fountain in the middle. The fountain's lines were obscured with snow, and a thin film of ice coated the edges. The boxwood hedges swept out in a great curve, following the lines of the carriageway, and stopped before they reached the house.

She was very aware of the silence as they trudged around the fountain. It was so *quiet.* Her breathing, though muffled by the weight of her scarf, seemed very loud. The crunch of her footsteps seemed to break through the silence like ice.

It's just the snow. Snow does strange things to sound, that's all.

The door loomed before them. Bryony had been stealing glances at it for some time and it kept getting taller and wider until when she finally arrived, it was nearly twelve feet high and wide enough for a hay wagon.

It didn't look ruined or abandoned or even very old. The door-handles gleamed, and a great iron shield in the middle, cut into the shape of a stylized rose, had not rusted. Only a thin rime of white clung to the edges.

Two bushes flanked the doorway, in great marble planters. The ugly stems with their wicked thorns were immediately obvious as dormant rosebushes. They had been pruned back heavily by someone who knew what they were doing.

A row of short marble steps led up to the doorway. Bryony dropped Fumblefoot's reins, hoping that the butler or the major-domo (if there was someone there) could tell her where the stables were, and went up the stairs carefully, getting both feet on one before attempting the next. It would be just her luck to find the only hidden manor house in a thousand miles of woods, and then slip on the last step up to the door and brain herself on a marble planter.

She reached up to the door knocker and the moment her fingers touched it, the door swung silently open.

The hinges did not creak. There were no ominous noises. The door just swung open a little way and stopped, standing wide enough for a woman and a pony to walk through.

"Um. H-h-hello?" Bryony poked her head inside, hoping to catch someone in the act of pulling the door open.

There was no one there.

She couldn't even blame a well-weighted door this time, because the knocker was on the right and it was the left-hand door that had swung open.

The double doors opened onto an entryway as large as her own cottage, with a thick red carpet on the floor. Four doors led off in various directions, and a set of crystal sconces held beeswax candles, burning as brightly as if they had been lit a half-minute before.

As she watched, the door directly across from her swung slowly open.

At this moment, had she not been in imminent danger of freezing to death, Bryony would have turned around, climbed onto Fumblefoot's back, and ridden as far away as she possibly could. This was magic, no doubt about it, and the very *best* possibility was that somewhere there was a sorcerer who was going to get very annoyed when he found that a soggy peasant and her disgraceful horse had invaded his spotless domain.

The rather worse explanations involved wild magic or fairies or any number of things that meant this house was a great big trap and if she stepped inside, the door was going to slam shut and the house was going to devour her.

On the other hand, it was *warm* inside the house. Just being out of the wind left her feeling a hundred times warmer. She pushed her cloak hood back from her face.

I'll go back outside. We'll crouch down behind the wall, maybe, out of the wind—surely that'll be enough—I mean, I don't need all my toes, and it's better to lose a few than get eaten by a house—

It was so very warm. She hadn't been dressed for a blizzard, but even her light cloak and gloves were starting to feel hot.

"Hello?" she called again.

No one came. If there was a butler, he was invisible, and wasn't that a pleasant thought?

Bryony stood on the threshold in indecision, until something shoved her hard in the back.

She let out a yell and stumbled forward, sure that the door would slam and the lights would go out and then she'd start hearing something—a sound, a monster, something terrible—and she reached out to catch herself because her feet had gone cold and clumsy. She landed on her knees on the carpet with her head bowed as if waiting for the headsman's axe.

It had been Fumblefoot.

He whuffled at her worriedly when she fell down. Fumblefoot did not understand humans very well, except that some of them gave you grain and called you a good little idiot and some of them attached very heavy things to you and hit you to make you run. He knew he preferred the former to the latter, but his experience did not encompass humans that yelped and fell down when you poked them.

He shifted nervously from foot to foot. He was cold. There was warmth. What was going on?

"Idiot," muttered Bryony. She got slowly to her feet. The ice on her eyelashes was melting and streamed down her face like tears.

Horses were notoriously sensitive to magic—horses bespelled to have matching coats were wild and jittery for weeks afterwards—but with a real numbskull like Fumblefoot, you couldn't be sure. He wasn't even scared of barking dogs, because he didn't think they had anything to do with him. Magic might go right over his empty little head.

He didn't seem nervous. Hopefully that was a good sign.

"Well, I suppose if it's certain death or a magic house…"

It was possible that there was random benevolent magic scattered through the world. You heard about it occasionally. Groves where lost sheep turned up, springs that healed, trees that sheltered the hunted from the hunter.

It was just that you heard so much *more* about the nasty things that ate you in the dark.

She gathered up Fumblefoot's reins and led him into the house.

CHAPTER THREE

"Stay right there," Bryony told the pony. "If this is some sorcerer's house, we're not going to get hoofprints all over his nice floor. He's going to be mad enough as it is."

She pulled her scarf down. Her face was wet underneath, from her own breath steaming against the fabric. When she pulled her gloves off, her fingers were white, but she knew they would turn red and begin burning like fire any second now.

She turned back to Fumblefoot, thinking to pull his packs off and start rubbing him down, and saw that the double doors had swung shut.

Running was currently beyond her, but she stomped to the door, leaving bits of compacted white snow behind her, and pushed against it. Her heart was in her throat, because if it refused to open, she was going to have to panic, and she truly did not think she had the energy left.

It swung open easily, affording her a glimpse of the snowy world outside.

Bryony let out a long breath. Very well, then. They would be allowed to leave—or there was at least an illusion they would be allowed to leave—

Stop. This is too complicated. I cannot keep waiting for something to jump on me from the shadows when I am ready to fall down already. I will just trust that the house will let us go again, because there is nothing I can do about it if it won't.

She turned back, to find that Fumblefoot was investigating the open door.

"No! Stop, idiot!" She hurried to him and laid a hand on his shoulder, trying to push him away from the door. "You'll get snow all over the floor—the sorcerer'll kill us—if there is a sorcerer—oh, stop, stop!"

Melting snow was sliding off the bags and his tail and the saddle blankets and plopping on the thick red carpet. A trail of soggy hoofprints led from the door, and as she watched, he lifted his tail and—

"Oh dear God, no, *stop!*"

Fumblefoot gave her a reproachful look. Stop what?

I have broken into an enchanted manor house and my pony has crapped on the floor. Oh God. Bryony fought the urge to giggle hysterically. She would have to find something shovel-like—maybe she had something in the saddlebags—and then she could scoop the mess up and dump it outside. Her gloves would never be the same, but arguably neither would the carpet.

Fumblefoot took advantage of her distraction to go through the open door. Bryony gave the pile of pony droppings a guilty glance—they probably weren't going anywhere, after all—and hurried to catch him before he made even more of a mess.

The door led to a long hallway, built to a scale so impressive that even a pony in the middle of it did not make it seem significantly smaller. It was lined with doors and enormous oil paintings, decorative marble tables and wrought-iron candlesticks.

Everything was silent inside the house. It was as quiet as the snow-covered landscape outside. The carpet muffled her footsteps, and even the pony's thudding, squelching progress was muted. If she hadn't been able to hear him breathing like a bellows, she would have thought that her ears had frozen in the cold.

She reached under Fumblefoot's chin and snagged his reins. He let out a colossal sigh and tried to lean on her, and while she was avoiding being squashed against a marble-top table, a third door swung silently open in front of them.

The pony made for it so determinedly that he practically dragged Bryony along with him. Reins really only went so far with Fumblefoot: his previous owner had been a very bad man and left the pony with a mouth like iron, so he was fully capable of ignoring somebody hauling on the bit when he chose.

"The floors….!" said Bryony hopelessly. Her fingers were burning so badly that she couldn't keep a grip on the reins anyway, and let go to keep from being swept into the doorframe. She cradled her hands against her chest, and so it was hunched and nearly weeping in frustration that she entered the enchanted parlor.

There was a brick fireplace on the wall, and in the fireplace, a fire was burning. As soon as she saw it, she heard it as well, snapping over the logs and crackling through bits of kindling.

It was too much. The sight of the fire wrung the last energy from Bryony. Exhaustion poured into her bones like molten lead, weighing her down until she thought her knees would buckle.

Fumblefoot had found something to eat. "Because it is completely and totally normal for people to have buckets of hot mash in their parlors," said Bryony, to his ears. One flicked at her as if she were a fly.

She dragged the saddle off his back and managed to pull him out of the mash long enough to pull the bridle off his head. She had just enough strength to heave the saddle to one side. Her saddlebags went *clink,* because Elspeth had sent jars of liniment and preserves home with her, but nothing broke.

There was an elegantly laid table a few feet from the fire. Silver candlesticks burned amid piled fruit and covered dishes. Light rippled from the tablecloth in the way that light ripples from *very* expensive damask and doesn't ripple from anything else.

There was a single chair and a single place setting. Bryony didn't dare sit down. She pulled the elegantly folded napkin from under the gleaming silverware, turned back to Fumblefoot, and began rubbing his legs down with it.

Fumblefoot ignored her, slobbering happily into his food. Bits of grain and horse drool stained the carpet.

"It's their fault now," muttered Bryony, working her way down his hind leg with the napkin. "*They* gave him the mash." She had no idea who *they* might be—if it was a sorcerer, it was a very accommodating one. She supposed it could still be fairies, in which case Fumblefoot, having eaten fairy food, was probably trapped forever inside the fairy mound or ring of stones or...ring of boxwood... thing...poor fairies, they probably expected better...

She fell asleep next to the fire, with the battered napkin still in her hand.

Bryony woke up because her feet were finally warm enough to become excruciatingly painful.

She bit her lower lip and was just thinking that she needed to take her boots off and take a look at the toes in question when she realized that she had tucked the toes of her right foot up under her left knee, which would be very difficult if she were still wearing boots.

She opened her eyes. There was a blanket over her, and her boots were sitting next to the fire. Her cloak was hanging on a coatrack by the door.

Her first instinct was to sit bolt upright and look around for whoever had draped the blanket over her and pulled her boots off.

There wasn't anyone there. Fumblefoot stood in the corner, drowsing, on a pile of straw. (Clearly piles of straw were accessories in all the best parlors.) He lifted his head a little when he saw her move, then dropped his nose again with a contented *hurrff!*

"Right..." said Bryony. "Right...right. Okay. I can't have slept long. My feet are still cold." She gritted her teeth and pulled the blanket back.

She was still wearing socks. They were wet and squishy and regrettable. She yanked the socks off and laid them carefully across the hearth, then took a deep breath and looked down at her feet.

Her feet were bright red and burning so fiercely it made her eyes prickle—but none of the toes were purple or black or any odd color, and she could wiggle all of them.

The pain of moving them made her want to howl, but she wasn't going to lose anything to frostbite. A weight that had settled in the pit of her stomach seemed to lift. It wasn't that she cared that much about the toes, but the act of actually having them chopped off or fall off or whatever happened when you got frostbitten toes was so gruesome she'd been trying not to think about it.

She got up. She'd been lying on the floor in front of the fire, under a quilt covered in patchwork roses. There was a sofa on the far side of the room with thick pillows that looked much more comfortable than the floor.

Her bare feet made no noise in the deep pile carpet. As she walked toward the sofa, trailing the quilt behind her, the table full of food caught her eye again.

Her stomach growled.

"I'll be trapped forever in fairyland," she told her stomach. Her stomach did not seem to care.

Bryony wrapped the quilt around her shoulders, feeling like an invalid. The silver bowls glittered. The smell of fresh bread nearly drowned out the smell of horse and drying socks.

Well, if they wanted to trap me, it's not like they didn't have plenty of chances already....

It was a small, round loaf on a little wooden board. It was still warm from the oven, and how was that even possible?

Does it matter?

Her stomach insisted that it didn't.

She sank into the chair and tore off a hunk of bread. Her hand shook as she buttered it. The butter knife was heavy and the handle was intricately worked with a pattern of vines that ended in a swirling open rose.

"I am beginning to see a theme here," said Bryony dryly, and then didn't say anything more as she stuffed the bread into her mouth.

It was sourdough. It was incredible. She found that tears were leaking down her cheeks for no reason, and this was infuriating, because she hardly ever cried. She wiped the side of her hand across her eyes and looked around for more bread.

There were other things on the table. Bryony didn't quite have the energy to investigate the covered dishes. There were too many and they were too shiny and reminded her too much of meals in the capital. Besides, there might be something horrible under those covers—vipers or severed heads or something.

Anything is possible.

She cut a wedge of cheese and sandwiched it between more hunks of bread. It was soft and nutty and a great deal better than the cheese that her sister Holly so painstakingly coaxed out of goat milk.

A bunch of grapes lay beside the cheese. Bryony eyed them with suspicion. It was spring. Grapes would not be ripe for months yet.

When she and her sisters had lived in the capital—when her father had still been alive—there had been hothouse grapes all winter, as plentiful as apples and as little regarded. You could pick three grapes off a bunch and toss the rest away without even thinking about it. She had not seen grapes in midwinter for five years. The nuns in Longfarthing had an orangery, but the oranges were reserved for the sick, and if they grew grapes, no one outside the convent had ever heard of it.

She poked a grape. The skin was firm and green, with a faint reddish bloom. It did not shriek or run away or turn into a frog or do anything to advertise its magical origin, but surely it must be magic. Everything was magic. There hadn't been a pile of straw in the corner when they entered the parlor, and boots did not take themselves off, not with that many laces.

In the end, she left the grapes alone. The bread and the cheese could have had a mundane origin, but there was no way the grapes were anything but magical. And if fairies could doom you to a lifetime in fairyland by eating mere bread and cheese, then the odds were so stacked against mortals that there was no hope for anyone.

By the time she was halfway through her third cheese sandwich, Bryony was yawning as often as she was chewing. She pulled the rose quilt around her shoulders and stumbled to the sofa.

The cushions were deeper and softer than her mattress back home. She made it halfway through the thought *I wonder if the snow is still...* and fell straight down into sleep.

CHAPTER FOUR

Bryony woke for the second time and knew that the snow had stopped.

She wasn't sure how she knew, because there were no windows in the parlor, but something had changed. The house was still silent, but the quality of the silence was somehow different.

Well, I can always tell at home when it's stopped, without looking out a window. I guess it's no different here.

Relief swept through her, and a restless desire to be gone. They could leave. When the sun was up, they could find their way to the main road, and be free of this strange house altogether.

"Not that I'm not very grateful," she said out loud to the house. "I am, truly. You've saved our lives. If there's…um….anything I can do to repay you…"

She trailed off there. It was hard to think of anything that a gardener and her pony could do for an enchanted house. It probably even weeded its own flower beds.

She was eager to be up and going, but before she had even struggled free of the rose quilt and the deep sofa cushions, the smell of bacon hit her.

Her feet took her to the table without any conscious input from her brain. There was more bread, more cheese, and on the plate, neatly arranged on either side of a fried egg, were four strips of absolutely beautiful bacon.

"Oh God," said Bryony, sinking into the chair. "I'm not made of stone…"

It was thick and smokey and just chewy enough to be marvelous. Pigs would be honored to die if they could be assured of turning into bacon of this caliber. Bryony devoured all four strips and turned her attention to the egg and another loaf of bread.

At last, she leaned back in the chair and let out a contented sigh. She could get used to magic, if it cooked like this.

In a small vase to one side of the table, a rose had spread its petals. With the bacon gone, Bryony could smell its scent—a deep muskiness, as profound a rose scent as she had ever encountered. No other flower in the world smelled quite like that.

Bryony herself was not passionate about roses. Even in Lostfarthing, every cottage had its rosebush, and there were people who devoted every square inch of dirt not dedicated to vegetables to their roses. She wasn't one of them. A rambler had come with the house and had conquered a section of the back fence, and there was a decent-sized rosebush by the barn that had served as a home to uncounted generations of mockingbirds, but that was as far as it went.

It was perfectly possible, Bryony felt, to have enough roses and want to plant some meadow sage and bee balm to round things out instead.

Still, it was a lovely rose. Her sister Iris might like it. Iris was always bringing cut flowers in from the garden, and she suffered a good bit in spring, during that interminable stretch when the crocus had finished blooming and nothing else had taken its place. Bryony herself felt that the green haze of leaves at the base of last year's stems was far more glorious than any cut flower, but you really had to be a gardener to appreciate that sort of thing.

It was a magical rose, clearly. Even Bryony's enthusiastic rambler was only pushing out leaflets and had not manifested any buds yet. Still, all flowers were a little magical, weren't they?

Perhaps being magical means that it wouldn't wilt on the way home.

She pushed back from the table and washed her hands in an ewer of water. Then she saddled Fumblefoot. He was feeling frisky—or as frisky as he ever got—and mouthed at her sleeve, looking none the worse for his snowy adventure the day before.

Bryony tidied up as best she could, folding the quilt and stacking the dirty dishes, then pulled on her now dry socks and boots. She surveyed the room. "Well. Thank you again. For the fire and the mash and the bacon. We're very grateful." She cleared her throat a little.

There was an unused jar in the saddlebags. She poured an inch of water into it and transferred the rose into the jar. Once she got outside and mounted, she could find someplace to tuck it so that it wouldn't splash about too badly or get crushed. Iris worried much more than her other sister, and it would be a good peace offering for having been gone all night in the snow.

And admit it—it's also proof that this happened at all! Because surely no one will believe you otherwise.

The door to the hallway opened at a touch. She led Fumblefoot through it and was pleased (and secretly relieved) to see that the puddles and the pony droppings had vanished in the night.

She stretched out a hand to the door to the entryway.

Something roared.

The sound came from all directions, the echoes battering down the hallway until it was impossible to tell the source. Perhaps the house itself was growling.

Fumblefoot jerked back against the reins and Bryony had to grab for them as the roar came again. The floor seemed to shake and at first she thought that it was an earthquake or an avalanche, for surely such a sound could not come from a living throat. Then it came again and there was a snarling to it and it fell down to a growl that shook her bones and rattled the candlesticks in their silver sconces.

This is it, thought Bryony. *This is the price I pay. I knew the bacon was too good to be true.* She grabbed Fumblefoot's reins tightly so that he would not bolt back down the hallway, because the inside of the house must surely be its hunting ground and they would have to go forward if they had any chance of escape.

She shoved hard against the door and it slammed back against the wall. The entryway lay before them.

Through the door we have to get through the door if we get outside perhaps there's a chance…

The door to the outside was open.

Standing in the doorway, a great black shape against the snow, was a Beast.

"Oh God," someone said, very quietly. "Oh God, oh God." Bryony agreed with the speaker very much, but would have been surprised to discover that it was herself. "Oh God."

The Beast was well over six feet tall and extraordinarily broad. That by itself would not have set him apart from mortal men but his head was set low and forward, like a boar's, and his heavily muscled neck rose into massive shoulders, covered in a wild mane of hair. The double doors stood wide, but he filled the space and left no avenue through which a woman and a pony could escape.

He roared again. There were words in it somewhere, but all Bryony could hear was the quiet voice saying "Oh God, oh God," in prayer and terror.

"The rose!" roared the Beast, the white of his teeth a slash against the shadows. "The rose!"

Fumblefoot reared.

Bryony would have sworn on the grave of her mother that Fumblefoot *couldn't* rear, the pony didn't have it in him, but the Beast was nothing any horse could understand. The leather reins left a smarting red line across her palm, and then Fumblefoot had whirled around and was charging down the hallway in a mad dash for escape.

No, idiot, no, you can't run, you're not good at it, you certainly can't run on a carpet with tables everywhere, oh God—

She heard him stumble. His knees were so scarred and broken from his years as a cart horse that he could hardly run in the best of circumstances, but he was up immediately and went blundering and crashing down the hallway.

Her anguish was so great that she had brought Fumblefoot here, that he might not only be eaten up by a monster but that his last minutes would be spent in blundering terror instead of lying down peacefully in the snow, that Bryony snapped her mouth shut. Somewhere inside her was anger, and that anger wrenched her head up so that she stared full into the face of the Beast.

The Beast's face was somewhere between bear and boar, a long bear's muzzle with the wicked curves of tusks, a boar's high and awkward forehead with the heavy brows of a bear. He had dark fur, fine and dense across his face, but the eyes that met Bryony's were as yellow as fire.

"*The rose must not leave,*" he growled, and the growl went on and on and filled up the entryway of the house until Bryony was drowning in it.

She dragged her eyes away from the Beast's face, down the length of her own arm. Her left hand seemed to belong to some other person. Certainly she wasn't the one holding a jam jar, half-full of water, with a rose in it, was she?

The hand was shaking. The water sloshed in the jam jar, and the rose rolled back and forth on its stem.

She thrust her hand out, stiffly, toward the Beast. "Take it," she quavered.

The Beast spoke over her head, as if to someone on the ceiling. "How dare you?" he growled. "You dare—you *dare*—"

It would have been very pleasant to stay detached. Perhaps if you weren't quite there, being eaten by a monster didn't hurt so much. But unfortunately she seemed to be regaining her wits and her hand undeniably did belong to her.

"I'm sorry," she said. "I didn't know it was your rose. That is, I knew it was, I didn't know you cared about it. It's just a rose.

There was cheese and bread and bacon, too. I ate that. I'm sorry. I thought I was supposed to. I can't give that back. Well, I could, but you probably don't want it now. Please don't kill me?"

She ran out of breath and stared back up at the Beast, who was gazing down at her with narrowed yellow eyes.

Perhaps her apology had mollified him a little, because when he spoke again, the growling had subsided to a low rumble. Bryony could feel it through the soles of her feet. "I do not care about the rest. Only the rose."

She said nothing. She could not think of anything else to say. Her legs were shaking and the shaking was traveling up her spine and into her stomach and she thought in a moment that she might be sick.

"Give it to me," said the Beast.

She held out the jam jar. She could not have taken a step towards the Beast to save her soul, but she leaned far forward, clutching the doorjamb for support. The water was still sloshing, and it sloshed harder as the Beast stepped forward to take it.

He loomed over her. Most of the light and all of the air in the room seemed to vanish. Bryony fought to breathe.

She felt that strange swimming detachment again, as his hand came toward hers, and settled over the jam jar. His fingers were three times the size of hers, and ended in blunt black claws.

He was wearing some kind of robe with long, loose sleeves. It seemed to Bryony that the Beast was very careful to keep from touching her, but the cuff of his sleeve brushed across her wrist.

"You will have to open your hand," said the Beast, in a low rumble, although he was perfectly capable of wrenching the jar from her hand, or her hand from her wrist, if he so chose.

"Ah," said Bryony. "Yes. Of course."

She opened her fingers. The Beast took the rose.

"Right," said Bryony, and fainted.

CHAPTER FIVE

When she woke, she was in the parlor again, on the sofa. She opened her eyes, saw a dark humped shadow crouched by her side, and closed them again immediately.

"I never faint," she said aloud. "I consider it revolting. I have no patience for women who faint." She pinched the bridge of her nose between her fingers.

"On the contrary," rumbled the voice of the Beast, "I felt that your skull bounced most charmingly on the carpet."

Perhaps she was having a nightmare, or an extended hallucination. Perhaps she was freezing to death in the snow even now, and this was a last fevered dream before she died.

Yes. That made a great deal more sense than that she was trapped in an enchanted house with a Beast who had roared at her and now had apparently decided to mock her.

"And the way in which you soiled yourself with terror was graceful in the extreme," added the Beast.

Bryony's eyes flew open and she sat bolt upright, ignoring the ringing in her ears and the immediate stabbing pain behind her eyes. "I did *not!*" she cried, and then the smell hit her, and she realized that she had.

"It is not right that I am going to be both dead and mortified," she told the Beast. "Either kill me now or give me a change of underwear."

He was kneeling down, which put his head on a level with Bryony's. His golden eyes were cool and sardonic and amused.

"I am not going to kill you. And I fear that I do not carry women's underwear about my person."

"You are *not* a gentleman!" cried Bryony. It was not that she was too furious to be afraid, it was that the fury was sitting on top of the terror and riding it like a horse.

"No," he said. "I am a Beast." He made a restless motion on the cushions with one clawed hand, and Bryony gulped.

She was going to have to look at him. It would be too obvious if she wasn't looking at him.

She looked. He was still a Beast. His face was an animal's face, but like no animal she had ever seen.

It's fine. It's fine. Don't be rude. That's how he looks. He hasn't killed you yet.

She would have said something else, whether to apologize or to insult him or to continue to beg for her life, when a thought struck her and drove everything else from her mind.

"Fumblefoot! Oh Lord—" She grabbed the back of the couch to haul herself upright.

The Beast rose gracefully to his feet and stepped out of her way. "If that is the name of your—for want of a better term—*horse*, he is unharmed. The house stopped him and is feeding him carrots."

It was strange how the Beast referred to the house, but as it was not so different from how Bryony herself had been thinking of the enchanted manor, she let it pass. "He was afraid," she said, feeling a bizarre urge to defend the wretched pony. "He is not much to look at, I admit, but he's had a hard life."

"Haven't we all…" said the Beast dryly. He gazed down at her, then sighed, a sigh like a horse or a cow or some other large animal, not like a human.

Well, perhaps not quite like a cow.

"I believe we have gotten off on the wrong foot," said the Beast. "I am sorry." He bowed, with both hands clasped in front of him. "Why have you come here?"

"It was the rutabagas," she muttered, trying to assess the state of the damage to her underwear and trousers, which was considerable.

The Beast's eyebrows were round patches of light-colored fur, rather like those of a dog, but they shot upward very expressively.

"Rutabagas?"

Bryony put her face in her hands. There was no salvaging her dignity. She had fainted and then wet her pants, and while the Beast seemed increasingly disinclined to eat her—perhaps he didn't like his prey marinated in their own urine—she still did not know what he intended. She wanted to leave, even if it meant riding home on a damp saddle.

Still, he'd asked. So she told him about the rutabagas, and the freak snow storm, and getting colder and colder and then finding the road.

"Ah," said the Beast. "Yes. If a traveller's need is great, they sometimes find their way here. It is part of the magic at the heart of this place. One of the magics, in any event. So that explains that."

He frowned. Bryony, who had almost managed to watch his eyes and not the rest of his monstrous features, shuddered. There were a lot of teeth encompassed by that frown.

"But you should not have taken the rose," said the Beast, with a hint of a growl.

"Then maybe you shouldn't have left it on the table," said Bryony.

The Beast inhaled sharply.

Oh, that was brilliant. Yes. Antagonize him. That will end beautifully.

Perhaps she could talk him into letting Fumblefoot go. The pony might be able to find his way home, and then at least her sisters would know something had happened to her.

Although they'll have no idea what. And how could they even begin to guess?

"Rutabagas. Hmmph." The Beast turned and stalked across the room to the fireplace. He stared into the fire for a moment, and said, without turning, "You are a gardener, then?"

"Yes," said Bryony.

"What do you know about roses?"

Bryony exhaled. "They're a lot more trouble than they're worth."

A strange sound came from the Beast, and his massive shoulders shook. It took her a moment to realize that he was laughing.

"I mean it," said Bryony, nettled. "They get black spot and mildew and cankers and rust. I don't know why anyone bothers with the fancy types. They smell nice, sure, but they take ten times as much work as anything else in the garden. I prefer sages. Nothing bothers a sage."

"Or a rutabaga?"

"Don't talk to me about rutabagas," said Bryony grimly. She wondered if she could towel herself off with one of the napkins on the table. "Do you plan to keep me here talking, er, my lord?" She wasn't sure what to call him. *My lord* seemed safest.

"I am afraid," said the Beast, turning back toward her, "that I plan to keep you here permanently."

Bryony stared at him fixedly, focusing on the bright yellow eyes. Her mind was numb.

"Because of a rose?" she forced out.

"Yes," said the Beast, "though not quite the way you think."

She put her hands to her face and gave a strangled laugh. "Imagine if I'd nicked the silverware!"

"Would you like to nick the silverware? We have a great deal of it."

"But not of roses, apparently!"

"I am sorry," said the Beast. "I have need of you."

"But I cannot stay with you," she said. "My sisters—the garden—they'll *starve!* And my plants—"

She loved her sisters very much and would have died for them gladly, but the thought of losing her garden, the long rows of vegetables and the wild edging of herbs and flowers, the great purple sprays of lavender and the soft fuzz of lamb's ear—that was a loss so great she did not have words to wrap around it.

"They'll starve," she said again, because she knew that only a gardener would understand her other grief, and there was nothing about the Beast to give her hope. "I am the one who grows all the vegetables—"

"Can they not learn?" rumbled the Beast.

"Oh no. Well, Holly could. Iris is useless for anything but embroidery, she is afraid of worms…Oh, I only hope they can learn quickly enough! We have worked so hard, we came from so little—" She raked her hands through her hair. "We have earned a little breathing room, but a bad harvest or a missing gardener—"

She stopped, aware that she was talking too much, keenly aware of how pointless it all was. The Beast, in his vast manor, could not possibly know or care what it was like to be so poor that a well-stocked root cellar was the only hedge against starvation. She knotted her fingers together and stared down at them.

She would not beg.

In the bright shadows of the fire, the Beast shifted restlessly and said, in a low earthen rumble, "Perhaps I can make it easier."

"You can let me go!"

He shook his great head. "I will give you a week to return to your sisters. Then you must come back to me, or I will come to fetch you."

Bryony's heart, which had risen a little, sank down to her toes. "Come and fetch me," she repeated tonelessly.

"The house will," said the Beast. "I cannot leave the grounds. The house, however…" He spread his clawed hands. "Even I do not know all that the house is capable of."

Strangely, she did not doubt him. She wondered vaguely how it would happen. Would she step outside the cottage and find her feet on the road leading to the iron gate? Would Fumblefoot lead her here when her hands faltered on the reins?

Would the house tear itself up from its foundations and go striding across the landscape on legs of masonry and mortar?

She put her face in her hands.

"I suppose that I can hardly stay inside the cottage for the rest of my life," she said dully. "And if the house comes for me, my sisters—"

She stopped. The notion of the house reaching out for her and catching Iris or Holly instead was too much to bear. Holly would try to fight and be killed, and Iris would cower in a corner and weep.

Iris had only barely recovered from the death of their father. Something like the Beast she might never recover from again.

"It is a large house," said the Beast. "You will have all that you desire. Books, fine clothes…"

"Swear that you will not hurt my sisters," she said fiercely, turning on him, not caring about the state of her clothes any longer, or that she was like a mouse making demands of a wolf. "Swear that if I stay with you, you'll leave my sisters out of this."

"I want nothing of them," said the Beast. "If you come back within a week, they shall never see me."

Bryony's breath hissed between her teeth.

"Then I shall stay," she said, and the realization that her garden was lost to her was a cut so deep that she wrapped her arms around her belly and her breath caught with it. Only the knowledge that the Beast was watching her, and that she did not want to show any weakness before her captor kept her from gasping.

Perhaps I will not have to stay. Perhaps when he has had what he wants—whatever it is—perhaps he will let me go. Perhaps I will find a way to escape.

I have brought this on myself. I knew that this was enchantment, and I went inside anyway. If this is the price I pay to keep it from touching my sisters, then so be it.

"Please," she said wearily, no longer able to focus on the big things, and so seeking refuge in the small ones, "are there any clean clothes to be had?"

"You will have to ask the house," said the Beast.

CHAPTER SIX

The Beast left her alone for a few minutes with a basin of water and some soap. When she turned around, there were dresses laid across the sofa, great frothy concoctions of silk and lace and seed pearls, and Bryony began laughing, with a great deal of bitterness to be sure, but still, laughter. That had always been her great gift and her besetting sin, that even in the darkest and most somber times, she had the urge to laugh.

She had very nearly disgraced herself at her father's funeral by laughing, but since laughter looks much like tears if you keep your face covered, she had managed to pull it off.

The dresses, though…

"Good lord, no," she said. "Oh dear. I'm sorry. There is nothing there that I can wear. I would need ten maids to do up the buttons on that one, and I plan to ride a horse home. Find me a robe that I can wear until my pants dry, and that will do very well for me."

She was talking out loud to a house. It was a measure of how wearing the day had been that this no longer seemed unusual.

When she went to the hearth to spread her wet pants and undergarments before the fire, there was a robe hanging from the coatrack, next to her cloak. She took it down. It was dark pink and made of some plush fabric that would undoubtedly pick up every speck of lint and stray hair in the world. At the moment, however, it was gloriously soft and she rubbed her cheek on a sleeve unselfconsciously.

"Thank you, House," she said. "Err…if you could see that my clothes dry quickly…I'm not sure if you do that sort of thing…"

There was no reply. Possibly that was for the best. If the house had started talking back, she might have started screaming, and she wasn't sure that she'd be able to stop.

The door swung open, and the Beast came through again. He looked at her robe thoughtfully, but did not comment.

He was carrying a small chest in his arms—or perhaps it was a large chest, but he made it look small. He set it down on the table (which was now devoid of either dishes or bacon) and motioned to her to open it.

"This is for your sisters," he said, as she flipped the latch open. "So that you need not worry that they will starve."

She opened the lid. Gold caught the firelight and woke highlights on the underside of the lid.

It was full of gold royals, the most valuable coin in the kingdom, stamped with the king's head and the royal coat of arms. The cottage Bryony shared with her sisters might be worth a half-royal, if the buyer was generous. The contents of the chest could buy all of Lostfarthing and half of Skypepper, and put a new coat of paint on the other half, at that.

"No!" said Bryony, stumbling back from the chest. "No—no, you can't!"

She clamped her arms around her midsection and thought that she might be ill.

The Beast stared at her with honest bewilderment, and she realized that she sounded like a madwoman, that for once the Beast might be the one acting rationally.

"It's too much," she said, forcing the words out. "When you have money like this, people take it from you. Things happen. It's not—I can't—" She took a deep breath and looked down at the carpet. "If my sisters have this, someone will steal it. The townsfolk will look after them as they are, but if they have this—people aren't good with money like this. It—it does things to people's heads."

She knew all too well what things money did. She fanned her fingers out, rejecting the chest, trying not to sound completely mad. "So, thank you, I'm sure you meant well, but *no.*"

"Hmmm," said the Beast, in a meditative rumble. "I see."

"Besides," said Bryony, daring to look up, "you cannot spend royals in Lostfarthing. They would have to travel halfway to the capital to find anyone rich enough to make change."

The Beast shut the lid. "I have never before met anyone with an aversion to wealth. Someday you will have to explain it to me."

Bryony snorted and let her arms fall to her sides. "I suppose we will have plenty of time, unless you plan to sacrifice me to the moon gods on the next equinox, or something equally nefarious."

"Don't be ridiculous," said the Beast. "The moon gods require virgin sacrifices on the *solstice*, not the equinox."

"They're twice out of luck there, then," said Bryony.

The Beast's face writhed into a mass of teeth and tusks, and Bryony had a bad moment when she thought that her virginity might actually be what he was after, for some unknown magical reason—*But damnit, he should have asked, not just assumed, and I'm not ashamed, it's not like I ever planned to get married anyway, and even if by some chance I did it wouldn't be to someone who cared about a thing like that*—and then she realized that he wasn't angry.

The Beast was smiling.

"I think we shall get along very well, Miss…what shall I call you?"

"Bryony," said Bryony. "And what shall I call you?"

"Beast," said the Beast. He stretched out a hand, not to touch her, but holding it palm up in a way that was oddly reassuring, despite the claws. "And have I not already said that no harm will come to you? There will be no sacrifices, virgin or otherwise. On this you have my word."

"Mmm," said Bryony noncommittally. She wiggled her bare toes in the pile carpet. *What is the word of a Beast worth? Well, he is a sorcerer, and they are said to keep their word…though what they actually promise you may be different than what you think they are promising...*

"As for your sisters, Miss Bryony, I am determined that you not fear that they will starve. Will this do, in lieu of gold?"

He opened the chest again. The coins still glittered, but more softly now, on copper pennies and a few silver talers. There was no gold inside the chest.

Bryony exhaled slowly. It was wealth enough to keep her sisters for several years, to buy the second goat that Holly had been wishing for, to build the loom that Iris had been wanting, but had not even suggested that they could afford. Somehow you could not quite imagine buying a goat with a gold royal. The gold and the goat did not belong together in the same image.

It was more than she would have earned, carrying her vegetables to market for many years.

Perhaps her sisters would be able to find their own ways to survive. Holly would likely marry—she was pretty and blond and vigorous and did not mind hard work—and Iris needed to marry *someone*, if only so that there would be someone to kill spiders and save her from dangerous earthworms. The coins would serve as a generous dowry, if nothing else.

She took a silver taler from the chest and turned it over. The stamped wheat sheaves gleamed at her.

"I think it will do very well," she said to the Beast. "Thank you."

"It is the least that I can do," said the Beast.

CHAPTER SEVEN

"You're alive!" cried Holly, hardly waiting for Bryony to dismount from Fumblefoot, and not bothering to open the gate before she scrambled over it. "You're alive, Iris thought you were dead, nobody's seen anything like that blizzard, not even Old Bran, but I knew you had to be alive, I said you probably stayed with Elspeth—"

"Yes, yes, I'm alive," said Bryony, getting down from Fumblefoot. The pony had been a bit edgy during their ride home, although that may have been from an overabundance of magic carrots, the house apparently having no idea that you were eventually supposed to stop producing them. "Let me put Fumblefoot in the barn, and then…well, I've got a lot to tell you."

And may God have mercy on me while I tell it…

She wasn't worried about Holly. Holly would overcome this the way she overcame everything. When they had lost everything and fled the city in disgrace, when their father had died during the long winter that followed, Holly had gotten up every morning and thrown herself into the next task at hand, sometimes not saying more than ten words a day, but still plowing grimly forward.

It was Iris who Bryony was worried about. She sighed.

Holly matched her step for step as they went back to the barn, where Fumblefoot lived with Blackie the goat.

"Something's up," Holly said, before they'd gotten halfway there. "You're not yourself. What happened?"

"I've been home two minutes," said Bryony, annoyed. "Couldn't I just be tired?"

"No. You're walking wrong. Like you're expecting somebody to jump out at you."

Holly had a cheerful pink face and big, twinkling blue eyes, and Bryony occasionally had to remind herself that her sister also had a mind like a handful of razors.

"I'd rather only tell it once," said Bryony tiredly. "You're not going to believe me anyway, either of you, and it'll be easier this way."

"I'll believe you," said Holly. "You're my sister. I don't think you've ever lied to me about anything important."

"I lied to you about who got punch on your favorite dress when you were twelve."

Holly waved this off as unimportant. "Yes, well, I dropped your doll down the well, so it all evened out."

"Mmm." Bryony unsaddled Fumblefoot and gave him a desultory rub down. They had come out of the woods less than a mile from Lostfarthing, despite the complete impossibility of doing so.

Holly hefted the saddlebags over her shoulder as they walked towards the house. Chickens clucked and wobbled out of their path. "Well, whatever it is, I'm sure it's nothing," she said.

"It's something," said Bryony.

"In that case," said Holly, switching shoulders, "just let me know who you want dropped down a well, and I'll see what I can do."

Telling her sisters did not go as well as Bryony had hoped.

She told the whole story through, sitting on a stool in front of the fire, with her fingers wrapped around a mug of peppermint tea.

At the end of it, Holly said "Huh!" explosively, and then there was a brief silence, and Iris burst into tears.

Holly rolled her eyes and dropped a shawl over Iris's shoulders. (It didn't stop the crying, but it did rather muffle it, and it usually calmed Iris a bit, like covering a birdcage.) Holly drew closer to

Bryony. "Now," she said, "if you say this is what happened, I will believe you. But I have one question first."

"Ask," said Bryony wearily, staring into her tea.

"Did you meet someone and fall madly in love and now you're running away with him to a better life and this was seriously the best story you could think of? Because if it is—"

"Oh God, if only!" said Bryony, and started laughing painfully, which only made Iris cry harder.

"All right, then," said Holly. Her eyes strayed to the little chest on the mantelpiece. "I will admit, the coins make compelling evidence…although he values you far too cheaply, if that's all he thinks you're worth…"

Bryony hadn't mentioned that the Beast had offered her gold. She made a noncommittal sound and took a sip of tea.

"So now that that's settled," said Holly, sitting back on her heels, "you obviously can't go back."

Bryony hadn't really expected them to cheerfully agree that she should march back into the hands of the Beast, but she was hoping to get Holly on her side, at least.

"But—"

"A strange man-monster lures you into the woods and informs you that he means to hold you prisoner? Are you mad? I shouldn't have to tell you this." Holly's eyes narrowed. "Did you hit your head? Is there something you're not telling us?"

"No, no—"

"Did he feed you poisoned food and if you don't come back in seven days, you don't get the antidote?"

"I—wait, *what?*"

"Are you enchanted?" Holly leaned forward and peered at her pupils.

"How would we tell?" asked Bryony, exasperated. "And the Beast did save my life—"

"Yes, yes, he's a great humanitarian." Holly waved this off, then paused. Her finger drifted to her lower lip. "Unless he *is* a humanitarian…and he's looking for a next meal…"

"I don't think he's a cannibal," said Bryony, wondering how they had gotten so far afield, "and anyway, if he wanted to eat me, he would have. He didn't have to let me come back and say good bye."

"But what if he means to kill you?" cried Iris, taking her hands away from her face long enough to hurl the words out, then immediately covering her face again.

"I don't think he does," said Bryony slowly. "I'm nearly sure of it. There's something else going on there. Something…something I can't figure out…"

"So what?" asked Holly fiercely. "Why do you have to be the one to figure it out? His house can grab people, he says—well, let him grab someone else!"

Bryony shook her head slowly. "I can't explain it. But I think the Beast is in trouble."

Holly snorted, and Iris looked out between her fingers long enough to give her sister a disbelieving look.

She couldn't explain it. If she tried, it would sound flimsy, and her sisters would drag it out and dissect it and make her see how ridiculous it was, and Bryony didn't want to hear it.

Because something strange *was* going on, even beyond the enchanted house and a Beast defensive of his roses.

When she had led Fumblefoot through the wrought iron gate, and prepared to ride away, the Beast had come out to meet her. Fumblefoot didn't like him and tried to dance nervously, but because it was Fumblefoot, he had to settle for a few sidesteps and a disgruntled whuffle.

"Give me your hand, Miss Bryony," said the Beast.

Bryony tried to read something in his eyes—the eyes, that was the trick, look at the eyes and not at the great tusked muzzle beneath them—but there was nothing.

He could have twisted my head off like a pigeon's at any point. It seems unlikely he'd put me on a horse and then yank my hand off.

She stuck her hand out, feeling foolish.

The Beast reached through the bars of the gate and took her hand in his own very large one. For a moment it looked as if he was the prisoner, not she.

He held her hand very lightly, with his thumb lying in a bar across her fingers, and said "Miss Bryony, please listen to me."

Bryony, who had been staring at the dark clawed hand wrapped around her own, looked up sharply, because on the word *listen* he had given her fingers a quick hard squeeze, like one who seeks to convey a secret message.

"You must come back in a week's time," he said, gazing intently into her face. "The house will come for you, otherwise. It has great power." He squeezed her fingers twice more, on *house* and *power*. "But I have no wish for you to be unhappy. Bring with you anything you need in your new life—mementos, hobbies, beloved objects. And as you are a gardener, please bring anything that you require—seeds for planting, tending, staking, pruning…whatever it is that gardeners do."

He dropped her hand dismissively as he said this last, but Bryony was more puzzled than ever, because he had given her fingers a final hard squeeze on the word *gardener,* and his golden eyes never left her own.

"Um," said Bryony. "Yes. I will?"

The Beast had nodded and turned away, stalking back towards the house. The folds of his robe spread out around him like a shadow on the melting snow.

"Hey," said Holly, flapping her fingers in front of Bryony's face. "Hey! Have you heard a word I've said?"

Bryony started guiltily. Iris had stopped crying in the corner, so probably more time had passed than she thought. "Sorry. Woolgathering."

Holly threw her hands in the air. "I'm making more tea," she said. "Clearly you're not going to listen to anyone tonight, but maybe tomorrow you'll be ready to hear reason. And in the meantime, there'll be tea."

Bryony's own cup had gone stone cold. She handed it over.

Listen. House. Power. Gardener.

Gardener? Really? How did that fit?

Gardening may be my great joy, but I don't delude myself that it's that important in the grand scheme of things…and why it would be important to the Beast, I can't imagine…

There was something more at work here. And if Bryony was going to be drawn into it, she was determined to get to the bottom of it.

CHAPTER EIGHT

The snow melted almost at once. When Bryony had led Fumblefoot to the barn, his hooves cut holes in the snow and struck mud underneath. By morning, those holes were twice as large and smaller holes had appeared everywhere, cutting the white blanket into lace.

By noon, it was gone entirely.

In the next few days, Bryony found herself thinking that the garden must know what was about to befall the gardener, because there had never been such a spring.

The fine haze of green leaves at the base of old stems became foot-high thickets practically overnight. The asparagus-like stems of false indigo came up like a forest of spears, and clover rioted down the pathways. Bryony felt as if she barely had time to sow a row of seeds before she had to turn around and begin thinning the seedlings, as if they threw their second and third sets of leaves in the moments when her back was turned.

The generosity of the garden humbled her. She could not shake the feeling that it was trying to take care of her, overflowing in every direction so that she had enough of everything to take with her. She lifted and divided and potted from dawn to dusk, begrudging every moment spent inside eating, or outside tending to the chickens.

"It looks like you're trying to take the whole thing with you," said Holly, bringing out a cup of tea once more, four days after Bryony had come home.

"Well," said Bryony, chopping her spade through a ball of tightly wound roots, and prying the smaller half out of the ground. "Well. I suppose I am, a little."

"You're going to miss the garden more than either of us," said Holly, and that was a statement, not a question, which was good. Otherwise Bryony would have had to answer, and it would almost certainly have been a lie.

"I'll miss you very much," she said instead, which was true.

"Ah, but we're only people, after all," said Holly, amused. There was no censure in her voice. Holly understood things. And then, more seriously, "Bryony, you don't have to go. If you stay here—whatever happens—we'll deal with it. I'll tie you to me with ropes, and if this Beast and his house comes for you, he'll have to take us both."

"And leave Iris all alone?" asked Bryony, transferring the roots, with their accompanying green spikes, to a waiting piece of burlap. "She'll be dead in a week." Iris had spent the last few days alternating between claiming that if Bryony stayed home and inside the cottage, she would be fine, and a deep conviction that the Beast was going to eat Bryony and then possibly the rest of the town. That she was able to hold both positions several times a day without seeing any contradiction was no longer a surprise to her sisters.

"She'll go into town to Widow Grayson," said Holly practically. "The Widow needs somebody to work the loom, now that her eyes are going, and she fancies Iris for that dim son of hers anyway."

"All the more reason for you to stay here," said Bryony. "Iris's fate would be far worse than mine. I just have to deal with an enchanted manor house and a somewhat sarcastic monster, not marry the Grayson boy."

Holly snorted. Bryony tied the burlap square around the roots of the plant, wet it down, and added it to a straggling row of similar burlap sacks.

"Why are you so determined to go?" asked Holly. "Truly?"

Bryony wiped her dirt-streaked hands on her trousers and sat down next to Holly. Her sister had brought out another cup of tea, and she gulped it gratefully, even when it burned her tongue.

"Do you remember the city?" she asked finally, when it became obvious that Holly was not going to be put off.

"Mmmm," said Holly, who remembered it the way that a soldier remembers a great and terrible defeat.

"When we'd lost…when Father had lost…well. You know." Bryony laced her fingers around her knee and leaned back. The sun was warm, and she could hear the rustle of leaves as the pea plants investigated the side of the house. "When everything was sold, and all we had left was a cottage so far away that nobody wanted it… I stopped feeling miserable. It was like I'd come out the other side. I remember this kind of crazy exhilaration as we left the city."

"Because we were finally leaving?" asked Holly, the teacup forgotten halfway to her mouth.

"A little. But more…" Bryony spread her arms. "If that could happen to us, if we could be rich and then suddenly have nothing—if life could change that much, overnight—then *anything* could happen. Birds could turn into fish. The sun could rise at midnight. I could learn to fly. The world was obviously wilder and stranger than anyone knew. And there was nothing left to lose. Nobody could take anything from us, because we didn't have anything left to take. I felt invincible."

"Hmmm," said Holly. She remembered the teacup and drained it. "I think I understand. When we left the city, on that rattletrap wagon, I remember thinking, 'Thank God, it doesn't matter anymore that I'm not pretty, at least nobody's going to pretend that I'm beautiful just because I'm rich.'" She wrinkled her nose. "When I realized that, I started laughing, because it was such a relief, and Iris thought I was crying and started up herself, and I couldn't explain without sounding completely mad."

"Oh, well, *Iris,*" said Bryony. She remembered when their creditors had come to cart the furniture away, including the marble-topped vanity in her bedroom, and she had thought, *No one will try to smother me in paint again, trying to interest some poor nobleman in a short and rather plain merchant's daughter.* It had been a different feeling, but close enough that she thought Holly probably understood.

Holly stood up and brushed dirt from the seat of her pants. (Both she and Bryony wore trousers around the farm simply because it was easier, although Iris said it was barbaric and wore long skirts even when feeding the chickens.) "You can't distract me, you know. What does our questionable mental state leaving the city have to do with your Beast?"

"He's not *my* Beast," said Bryony, nettled. "And it's the same feeling, you know? I feel like anything could happen. And I might be able to fly."

Her sister raked her hands through her hair and blew her breath out, sounding a bit like Fumblefoot when he was exasperated. "Well. If that's how it is, then that's how it is." She gave Bryony's shoulders a brief, fierce squeeze, which reminded Bryony oddly of the Beast's grip on her fingers. "It seems like you need to do this, so I won't stop you. And I'll try to keep Iris from driving you mad."

"Thank you," said Bryony gratefully.

Holly surveyed the line of burlap sacks and the green riot of the garden. "Just be careful. And come back to us as you can."

On the morning of the seventh day, Bryony loaded up Fumblefoot, said goodbye to her sisters, and went into the woods.

Despite what she had told Holly, her heart sank with every step of Fumblefoot's jarring stride. She had gathered her bundles up in the gloomy pre-dawn light, and the last sight of her garden made her throat tighten. Even plants that usually stayed dormant until well into May were thrusting up green shoots to bid her goodbye.

Only the roses, clawing across the fence and the side of the barn, stayed sullenly quiet, as if they now begrudged even the few reddish-brown leaves that they had unfurled. That was fine. Bryony was suspicious of roses now, and would have rooted them out if she hadn't thought that it would involve copious amounts of blood and swearing.

There had also been her sisters. Iris, with many tears, had pressed a dozen pouches on her, each one embroidered with a flower. "For s-s-seeds," gulped Iris. Bryony was absurdly touched. Apparently, while Bryony had slept, her sister had been awake, huddled by the fire, embroidering flowers. It was a more practical gift than she would have imagined Iris to be capable of.

Holly had waited until Iris had turned away, and then slipped a package into her hand.

"Keep it on your thigh," she muttered in Bryony's ear. "You can cut a slit in your skirts for it. If the Beast goes for you, make me proud."

Bryony had begun laughing, despite the gravity of the situation, despite Iris sobbing quietly on the doorstep, as much at the dangerous glint in Holly's eyes as at the fact that her sister had just given her a dagger.

Gont the blacksmith must have made it. It resembled one of the long knives the hunters carried, but lighter, with a hilt made for someone with smaller hands. You could gut a deer or a man with it, if you were so inclined. Bryony suspected that she was *not* so inclined, but then again, perhaps she'd simply never had the opportunity. Life had so far presented her with very few people to gut.

Possibly that was about to change.

She would have wondered how on earth her sister could afford it, but the blacksmith's interest in Holly was well known, and Bryony was fairly sure that interest was returned.

Well. At least she need not worry about how her sisters would be taken care of while she was gone. And since the knife made Holly feel better, Bryony carefully strapped it to her thigh, although she suspected that if she tried to pull it on the Beast, she would slice her own leg open and probably bleed to death.

Yeah, that'll *show him.*

She was a great deal more comfortable with her pruning shears, which were wickedly sharp and had a curved blade that could give someone a serious poking or chop their finger off, assuming that they were obliging enough to hold their finger out and allowed it to be so chopped. You had to saw a bit going through the tougher branches, presumably fingers wouldn't be any easier…

Fumblefoot stumbled and poked her reproachfully with his nose. He had so many plants and twigs and burlap-wrapped stalks tied to his back that he looked like a small hillside. They were not terribly heavy, although a pot full of damp soil could weigh a great deal more than one would think, but they were bulky and awkward, so Bryony had chosen to lead Fumblefoot instead of riding.

The Beast had assured her that it would be easy to find the house again. "Go into the woods," he said, "and the path will appear."

Perhaps he had been wrong, or perhaps the path had simply not expected her to get such an early start on the day. It was nearly an hour before the trees opened up, and Bryony found her feet on the path that ran beside the stone wall.

The Beast was waiting for her, on the other side of the gate.

He was more alarming than she had remembered, or perhaps Bryony had softened the less human edges in her memory. She had not recalled that his tusks were so large, or his eyes so yellow.

I've made my bed. Time to lie in it, I suppose.

His eyebrows rose when he saw Fumblefoot plod into view.

"Bones of the moon!" he said. "What is all of *that?*"

"You told me to bring what I needed to garden," said Bryony defensively. "That's plants. By definition."

"I was thinking of seeds," said the Beast, opening the gate. "And… I don't know. Trowels. Shears. Perhaps a shovel."

"You can't tell me that there is no shovel in this place," said Bryony. "*Everyone* has a shovel. Except we only have the one, and I didn't want to take it, because my sisters will need it."

"The house can probably come up with a shovel." The Beast took a few steps back, but Fumblefoot flatly refused to walk through the gate. Bryony sighed and began unloading him, setting the bundles and pots inside the wall.

"I did bring seeds," she admitted. "But some of these plants are my friends. I wasn't going to just leave them." She ruffled her fingers through the lavender.

"Oh good," said the Beast dryly. "Here I was afraid that I had kidnapped a sane person by mistake."

"If you are going to kidnap travelers, you will simply have to take what you can get," snapped Bryony. "If I don't meet your standards, I'd be happy to return home."

Which was true this morning, although it hadn't been completely true for several days prior. If the Beast sent her home, Bryony suspected that the mystery would nag at her until the day she died.

The Beast raised his hands in surrender. "I yield, I yield. You are a perfectly acceptable…err…victim. I apologize for having questioned you."

Bryony was not quite sure how to reply to this, so she changed the subject. "I need to send Fumblefoot back to my sisters."

The Beast eyed the pony with frank disbelief. "I question what crime your sisters could have committed to deserve him."

"Look," said Bryony, annoyed, "he may not be very impressive, but he can pull a cart if you're patient with him, and he's very good-natured, which is more than I can say for *some* people. And his previous owner had beaten him half to death trying to get him up a hill and Holly jumped on his back—the owner, not Fumblefoot—and nearly beat *him* half to death, and I gave him all the money we'd made that season for the poor bea—creature—and also promised him that Holly would leave him alone, and we had to live on potatoes for two weeks because of it, so he's *ours* now, okay?"

There was a brief silence. Bryony petted Fumblefoot's nose fiercely and told herself that she wouldn't look at the Beast. She hadn't meant to say the bit about the potatoes.

"Um," said the Beast. "I see. I had no idea. I, er, apologize. If you've unloaded him, then I'll send him back."

"Thank you," said Bryony. She checked to make sure that there was nothing to catch on any twigs or branches, and carefully looped the reins up out of the way. He was still wearing the saddlebags, but they were empty now. She checked the snaps to make sure they were all closed and wouldn't flap, then checked them again, because she was stalling.

"Be good, Fumblefoot," she told him finally, rubbing her sleeve against his cheek. "Be good for Holly." Fumblefoot lipped at her fingers and gazed up at her with a mild brown eye.

She stepped back. The Beast waited a moment longer, then moved up to the gate. The pony stamped a hoof and glared.

"Go home, Fumblefoot, and find your way safely," said the Beast, and laid an open-handed slap on the pony's rump.

Affronted, Fumblefoot broke into a trot down the roadway. His gaits were never very reliable, but Bryony didn't hear him stumble as he trotted away and out of sight.

"That should bring him safely home," said the Beast. "Unless a more powerful magic intervenes, and that's really quite unlikely. Very few powerful magics are concerned with ponies."

Bryony turned away and pretended to busy herself with the stack of pots. Her eyes were burning. It felt like her last link with home had just trotted away out of sight.

This isn't permanent. You'll find a way to escape, or the Beast will let you go when you've done whatever it is that he wanted you for. It's not forever.

"May I show you to your rooms?" asked the Beast, picking up the satchel that contained her few non-gardening-related possessions. "Do your plants need—err—immediate attention?"

He is trying to be polite. He may be a monster, but he is trying.

It made Bryony feel a little better. She straightened up and blinked a few times, fiercely, until the burning went away. "They'll keep until tomorrow. You will have to show me where I can dig my beds."

The Beast made a sweeping gesture with one arm. Now that the snow had melted, Bryony could see that the manor grounds on either side of the boxwood hedge were exactly as one would expect. *Rolling lawn and gravel paths, as far as the eye can see...* A second fountain reared off to the east, surrounded by shrubs clipped into aggressively geometric shapes.

"Anywhere," said the Beast. "Wherever it pleases you."

Oh dear, thought Bryony with dismay, eyeing the military precision of the grounds. *My garden is going to look very strange out in all that.* She tried to imagine the purple spires of meadow sage and the exuberance of lamb's ear. *It will be very untidy.*

Well, let it be untidy. The groundskeepers and I will figure something out...

Aloud she said "I will have to talk to your groundskeepers."

"There are none," said the Beast.

"What?" Bryony turned in a slow circle, waving a hand toward the boxwood. "Who keeps everything trimmed and pruned and mowed and—how? Places like this take a whole *army* of caretakers." She did not add, "And you could grow enough vegetables to feed a village with all that wasted labor," but she thought it.

"The house does it," said the Beast. "All of it."

"So who *does* live here?" asked Bryony, gazing up at the vast manor house. Ranks of windows marched across its face. It could have held the entire population of Lostfarthing, with an entire wing left over for unexpected guests.

"I live here," said the Beast. "And now you. That's all."

CHAPTER NINE

Perhaps the Beast is lonely.

That was the thought that Bryony kept returning to, all that long morning. It made a certain kind of sense, but she had a feeling that it was not the whole reason, or even a very large part of it.

People who were merely lonely did not try to send coded messages by squeezing your hand. Something deeper was afoot.

That the Beast was a person, Bryony did not even question, but then, she believed on some level that Fumblefoot was a person, and Blackie the goat, and the neighbor's large and grumpy tomcat.

It was not that she was sentimental about animals. Chickens, for example, were not people. You looked into a chicken's eyes and you saw the back of the chicken's eyeball.

The Beast, however, was definitely a person, even if he looked like a nightmare.

His feet made no sound as he walked. This was understandable on the carpet, where even Fumblefoot's hooves had been muffled, but then they came to the end of the corridor and a pair of glass doors that led into a tiled courtyard. Bryony's boots clomped on the tiles, but the Beast glided along as silently as snowfall.

In the center of the courtyard was a little open circle, where a bare white birch tree lifted its branches.

All around the base of the tree grew roses.

Unlike her sullen rosebushes at home, these were fully leafed out, little blunt ovals of green with dark red veins. There were flowers in every stage from barely budded to blowsy and dripping petals, all of them deep, dark scarlet. Small drifts of petals lay across the tiles.

She did not want to compare them to blood. It was a shame that there were so few dark red things in the world.

They're like…like very dark tomatoes. Or late sunsets. Or a very nice cut of raw meat.

Oh dear. Raw meat isn't much better, I suppose…

"This is where your rose came from," said Bryony.

"They are not *my* roses," said the Beast, and his voice was deeper and more gravelly than it had been. "They belong to the spirit of this place. They require no tending."

"Just as well," said Bryony, forcing a laugh. "I have no patience to tend roses."

The Beast led her across the courtyard. Bryony saw that the roses were twining around the base of the birch, the great roses shining against the white bark like—well, yes, like blood spatter on snow. In a few places, the stems had bit so deeply that the bark had begun to grow over them.

"They've been there a long time," she said.

"Yes," said the Beast, "a long time." The air made a little space around his words, in a way that was not entirely pleasant, and Bryony did not say anything more until they had left the courtyard.

Through another set of glass doors lay a staircase. It was as wide and grand as any Bryony had seen in the capital, lit by sconces, with a banister that looked perfect for sliding and a spiky finial at the bottom that looked perfect for impaling anyone who tried.

"Your rooms are at the top," said the Beast, nodding up it. "I suspect that you would like to rest a little."

She looked at him. "I've been awake for less than four hours."

"Collect yourself, then?" asked the Beast. "Err—powder your nose?"

Bryony suspected that he was trying to be kind, and took pity on him. *If we are indeed the only two beings in this house, apart from the house itself, which is definitely peculiar, and I am going to be here for any length of time, we will have to make an effort to get along together.*

"Very well," she said, taking her satchel. "Thank you."

"I have a regrettably sharp tongue," said the Beast, "and you likely already despise me for kidnapping you, but as there are only the two of us, I will endeavor to be a considerate—er—captor."

Since this ran perilously closely to her own thoughts, Bryony felt one corner of her mouth crook up. "And I suppose I will endeavor to be a considerate—er—victim. At least until I find a way to kill you and escape and so forth."

"Well, naturally," said the Beast, smiling a little. His tusks gleamed in the candlelight. "I would expect no less. If there is any way in which I may assist you with the killing and escaping and so forth, please let me know."

Bryony ascended the stairs. Halfway up she looked down, and saw that the Beast was standing at the bottom, still watching her.

"There is a lock on your door," he called, "if you wish to use it. I do not have a key to it, so try not to lock it and then fall and hit your head on the bathtub or something equally humiliating."

"I'll try to avoid it," she said. "Thanks for letting me know." What use a lock would be in a magical house that could open doors on its own, Bryony wasn't sure, but it was a nice gesture.

She was glad to reach the landing, which was overcrowded with decorative urns, and go up the second flight and out of sight.

At the top of the stairs was a round room with green wallpaper and three doors. The one in the far wall stood open, and over the top, in elaborate scrollwork, it read, "Bryony's Room."

Bryony stepped up to the threshold, leaned in, said "Oh *no!*" and began giggling helplessly.

Then the stress of the morning caught up with her, and she had to lean against the doorjamb with her hand over her mouth, laughing until tears came. When the tears threatened to turn into something else, she forced herself to stop.

"I'm sorry, House," she said to the air, "I suppose I will call you House, since I have to call you something, and a name like 'Bob' or 'Tom' doesn't seem quite appropriate. It is a very pretty room. It's just...well..."

It was pink.

The walls were pink, the floor was pink, the bedding was pink, even the furniture was rosewood and, while quite attractive, came perilously close to pink. There was a wallpaper border of pink floral designs, and the crown molding across the ceiling was white with a pattern of pink spirals, and the candlesticks were thorny black iron brambles, topped by iron roses with the candles rising out of them like stamens. There was a tapestry on the wall showing a bluebird perched among pink flowers and the dark pink carpet was broken up by a round rug in the shape of an enormous dahlia.

Which was also pink.

Bryony took several steps forward, around a decorative pink urn—House apparently liked urns—and gazed in dismay at the canopied bed. It stood on a little raised platform, like an altar or a stage. It could have held Bryony and both her sisters, and they could have slept the night through without ever encountering a stray foot or hand from one another.

Lace foamed over the bedskirts and pillows and down from the canopy like pink lianas. The bedposts were carved with climbing roses. There were silk hangings about the bed embroidered with more flowers, all in shades of red and pink and vermilion.

Bryony had never before had occasion to contemplate what it would be like to find oneself inside a uterus, but she suspected that sleeping in the bed would be rather like that. Except with more flowers.

She tried to find someplace to rest her eyes that was not pink and rose-filled, and settled on the bluebird. The splash of blue was her only anchor in the room.

"Right," she said aloud, to the house, or possibly the bluebird. "Um. Yes. Very...err...kind." Perhaps there would be some hangings elsewhere in the house to tame the intensity of the walls. She'd have to look. "Very…pink. Yes."

Two steps up onto the platform brought her to the bed. She looked dubiously at the space under it. The bedskirts hid the space underneath, but she had never liked beds with too much space under them, even when she was younger and had slept in a carved bedstead instead of on a straw-tick mattress. There was too much room for things to lurk. Merely because nothing had, in seventeen years, reached out and clutched her ankles didn't mean that it wouldn't happen someday if she let her guard down.

She dropped her satchel on the bed. The brown leather was another comforting spot in the sea of pink. Perhaps she could navigate from spot to spot, bluebird to brown satchel to the window on the far side of the room. There had been some celadon urns out on the landing. Possibly she could appropriate one or two.

She sighed. When the initial shock of the pink had faded, the grandness started to overwhelm her. There had been a time when she would have fit in such a room, but that time was long ago and very far away.

She trudged to the window. Normally, grandness would not have bothered her so much—Bryony had learned to be grimly proud of her relative poverty, because the alternative was to be crushed by it—but there was something about the Beast's manor that made you feel as if there was almost certainly dirt under your fingernails, and perhaps something unpleasant stuck to your boots.

She checked her nails, sighed again, and tucked her hands under her elbows. Very well. She was a gardener, after all, and there was no shame in dirt under your nails. None whatsoever. If the house was going to be judgmental about it, it could go hang.

The window beckoned. Bryony peered out and felt her sprits lift a little, because it overlooked the birch tree. The bare branches had not yet leafed out, but they were a shape that she understood, and which did not make her feel small and grubby and out of place. Birch trees were the same tree no matter who you were. Even the very rich did not get better birch trees.

"I wonder if I could set some of my pots in the courtyard," she mused. "The roses are very nice and all, but it could use some lavender and some phlox. Something to mess it up a little."

The Beast had said that she could make her garden wherever she liked. Much of it needed to go directly into the ground, but surely she could keep a few in pots. Perhaps House could sacrifice a few urns to the cause.

She looked around the room. There was nothing that she needed to do right now. She could go and find the Beast again, see what he had planned for her, or perhaps go and scout out the grounds for a place with good sun and decently drained soil…

A movement caught her eye. One of the wardrobe doors swung silently open.

Bryony took a step back—*this is it, now the monster comes out and eats me*—but there were only dresses.

Lots of dresses.

Dresses with seed pearls and fur and tiny glittering gems and wispy skirts and very full skirts and puffed sleeves and slashed sleeves and leg-o-mutton sleeves and Bryony wasn't entirely sure that she wouldn't have preferred the monster.

"Oh dear," she said.

When she looked away, there was a particularly excessive dress laid across the bed. It had dark green stripes and the frothiness of the petticoats rivaled that of the lace on the bed.

"Oh, House…" said Bryony, rubbing a hand over her face. "House, are you trying to say I'm underdressed?"

When she took her hand away, a tiara set with tiny cut emeralds and a necklace as wide as a horse collar had joined the dress on the bed.

"I'm going for a walk on the grounds, House," she said.

The wardrobe door seemed to sag on its hinges and the candles flickered mournfully. Bryony closed her eyes.

I am making an enchanted house sad. God help me.

The skirt had been spread out to show elaborate stitchery. There were now two emerald bracelets wider than Bryony's thumb. Bryony sighed from the bottom of her toes.

And then, because there was something sadly hopeful about the dress, Bryony said, "When I come back, I promise, I'll dress for dinner."

The wardrobe doors clapped shut cheerfully, and the candles flared up in their sconces. Apparently this was acceptable to House.

There was an ewer of water on a low table by the wall. The basin was blessedly white but there was a pattern of pink stars around the rim. When Bryony poured out the water, it was warm. There were small white soaps and the towels were softer than any clothing that she had worn since leaving the city.

She made a half-hearted effort to get the dirt out from under her nails. The dirt laughed at her.

In the end, she settled for washing her face and hands, and then fled the over-pink room and the over-hopeful dress and went in search of the Beast.

CHAPTER TEN

She found herself unwilling to leave the rooms that she was familiar with. Who knew what House might get up to, in the far wings? Did it decorate and undecorate rooms to please itself? Were there storerooms holding dresses and buckets of mash and pink robes, in case they might be needed?

When Bryony had gone down the large staircase and opened the door to the little parlor in the front hall (which was neat as a pin and bore no trace of having briefly been a stable) and wandered through the courtyard without seeing any sign of the Beast, she gave up hope of finding him and went out to see her plants.

What had been a very large burden for Fumblefoot made a pathetically small knot against the vast sweep of lawn. Bryony felt a brief rush of indignation for her plants. They were good plants! How dare that lawn make them seem so trivial?

"I shan't feel guilty about tearing you up at all," she informed the lawn. "Even if I can't get very much of you at first. Hmm. I wonder if House can make decent manure?"

This led to a brief, searing mental image of the manor house lifting one massive wing and leaving a pile the size of a haystack behind it. Bryony giggled and hefted one of her purple sages in her arms, grabbed her trowel, and set off.

"The corner," she said. "By the wall, I think, so that I can have a little shade for those who need it, and so that I am not looking at that awful lawn from every angle!"

It was a long way. She shifted her grip on the sage several times as her arms got tired. The grass muffled her footsteps as thoroughly as the carpets inside the house had. Perhaps it was not grass at all, but green carpeting. It was unnaturally green for the time of year, and there were no brown spots anywhere. No weeds marred that perfect surface.

Perhaps I am the weed here. I am certainly unruly and rather common these days....although I wasn't always common. Perhaps my family is like one of those plants that starts out large and showy, but in a few generations the seeds revert to wild again.

She bowed her head. The sage brushed its leaves apologetically across her face, and the scent cheered her.

On the other hand, if we had stayed in the capital, it might have been many years before I had a garden of my own where I could get dirt under my nails and not have gardeners hovering around insisting that the young mistress not exert herself. What a lot of wasted years that would have been!

She and the sage reached the corner of the stone wall. Bryony set her plant down and began to pace out the likely dimensions of her new garden—a broad crescent of flowers here, and two straight rows of vegetables here, and a round bed in the middle for an herb wheel. That would probably do for now.

Using the edge of the trowel, she cut a line in the turf. It yielded smoothly to the touch of metal. The ground underneath was chocolate-colored loam, with streaks of red clay.

Bent over, her back already complaining, she cut the outlines of her bed in the grass. It went more easily than she'd expected. (Surely she was imagining that the turf pulled its roots away from the trowel like a lady pulling her skirts back? Although in this place, who could be sure?)

When she finally straightened, she was surprised at how much she'd gotten done, and a little discouraged at how much she had left to do. This was going to be shovel work, and a lot of it.

"I wonder if I have to go back to the house for a shovel, or if it can produce one out here?" she asked aloud, talking to herself, or possibly the sage.

"Close your eyes and ask it," suggested the Beast.

She whirled around. He was standing a few feet behind her, his clawed hands thrust into the pockets of his robe. She had not heard him approach.

"You startled me!"

He took a step back. "Forgive me. I should have called out." He spread his hands. "It has been some time. One forgets the niceties."

Bryony had not been expecting an apology. "Oh. Well. It's your manor, after all."

The Beast made a noncommittal sound.

"Is this—do you object?" She waved a hand at the newly outlined garden, and the lone sage plant sitting plunk in the middle of it. "You said I could put it anywhere."

"I meant it," said the Beast. "You can tear up the entire lawn if you wish." He gazed down at her handiwork. "Is this all?"

"All for this season," said Bryony. "I imagine, depending on how long I am to stay, that I may expand it."

The Beast said nothing.

After a moment, Bryony wiped her hands on her pantlegs and said "You said I should close my eyes and ask for a shovel?"

"I find it easier," said the Beast. "The house will make whatever you ask, if it can, but magic is...not always comfortable to watch. It will put it behind you, most times, but if you close your eyes, it will often be right in front of you."

Feeling a bit foolish, Bryony closed her eyes and said "May I have a shovel please, House?"

"Ah," said the Beast, sounding pleased, "there you are."

She opened her eyes, and a shovel was leaning against the wall. She picked it up and found the handle smooth and contoured. The blade was already sharpened, which was a great relief—sitting with a file trying to put a bit of edge onto a shovel was one of the least pleasant parts of gardening. She set it against the grass experimentally and stepped on it, and felt it sink smoothly into the ground.

"Before you begin digging your escape tunnel," said the Beast, "would you like a tour of the grounds?"

She raised an eyebrow. He was smiling, she thought, although it was mostly around the eyes.

"Certainly," she said, setting down the shovel. "There may be an even better place to escape from."

"This way, then," he said.

She took a few steps toward him, and found herself reluctant to get any closer. Certainly the last few feet would make no difference in how dangerous he was. He could take two strides and twist her head off, probably before she knew he'd moved.

It was simply that he was so very large, and there was an aura around him like the air before a thunderstorm. Bryony felt that her lungs were working harder to breathe the air around him, and was grateful when he began walking and she could fall back a pace without being obvious.

"How are your rooms?" asked the Beast.

"Oh," said Bryony. *Dreadful,* she thought. "Very…err…pink. And grand. But mostly pink."

"You don't like pink?"

"I shouldn't think anyone likes pink as much as that room does," said Bryony. "I've seen color-themed rooms before. There was a friend of my father's who had a suite done entirely in cloth-of-gold, but it wasn't quite so…so…" She waved her hands, unable to come up with a description that did not involve uteruses, and that was not a conversation she wished to start with the Beast.

"Your father had very wealthy friends, then," said the Beast. "For a gardener of Lostfarthing."

Bryony froze. The Beast stopped walking and turned his head toward her.

"You are looking at me," he said, "with eyes like an animal in a trap. It does not suit you, so we will assume that cloth-of-gold is found in every front parlor in Lostfarthing and there is nothing extraordinary about it. If the pink troubles you, you need only ask the house to change it. I expect that it would be willing to compromise."

"Compromise," said Bryony, finding her voice with difficulty. "Mauve? Or lavender, perhaps?" She shrugged. "I shall try to drag some other colors in, and perhaps it will mute the pink somewhat. I don't want to hurt its feelings."

As soon as she said it, she thought that this was a foolish thing to say. Did an enchanted house even have feelings? But the Beast nodded gravely.

"It is wise not to hurt the house's feelings."

For a moment the silence around them seemed to sharpen. When she looked up at the house, she half-expected to see it bent toward them, listening.

The moment passed. They came around the back of the house. More lawn, more hedges. Off in the distance, marking the lines of an old carriageway, were rows of chestnut trees.

They had nearly reached the carriageway when Bryony, who could see to the far wall by now, said "No vegetable garden."

"No," said Beast.

"What do you eat?"

The Beast shrugged. "The house creates the food, as it created your shovel."

Bryony shivered, remembering the bacon and the grapes. "And that…works? You don't starve? It's real?"

The Beast nodded. "The things it creates are real enough. If you take your shovel outside the gate, it will still be a shovel. The coins that I gave you for your sisters are not fairy gold, and will not melt away."

"Magic," said Bryony, who hadn't even thought to worry about the coins.

"Yes." The Beast spread his hands. "But if you grow a plant to eat—a tomato, or a lettuce or even a rutabaga—"

"Ha."

"—it is made of sun and earth and water. The house is much the same way. In fact—"

The listening silence settled upon them again, a silence so thick that Bryony could hear her heart beating in her ears.

The Beast snapped his mouth shut. She heard the click of teeth, and the rustle as he shifted from foot to foot.

It's his fur against his clothing. That's the sound. And that other sound is me running my hands over my trousers, and that's the calluses catching on the fabric, and I'd scuffle my feet in the grass but I don't think I'd hear it because the grass is part of this place and I think it's listening to us talk.

I don't like this.

It faded again, more slowly this time.

"Forgive me," said the Beast. "There are things I should not speak of. I do not mean to alarm you."

"I'm not alarmed," snapped Bryony. "Troubled and homesick and more than a little angry at being kidnapped—but not *alarmed.*"

"Good," said the Beast. "Hold on to that for as long as you can."

CHAPTER ELEVEN

He left her at the front gate. "I shall see you at dinner," he said, and bowed, then turned and strode away.

Dinner. Well. I suppose it's possible that he's waiting to eat me in a more civilized fashion, but this seems a terribly roundabout way to do it.

Bryony picked up another plant and trudged with it over to the garden. Her earlier enthusiasm had drained away. Now she just felt like an ant crossing the endless lawn, with the strange house hunched over her, listening.

She had moved a half-dozen plants and was starting to sweat when it occurred to her to ask House for a wheelbarrow.

After that strange silence earlier, she wasn't entirely sure that she wanted to ask House for anything, but still, it made all the food, and if she had to live on the proceeds of her garden, it was going to be a week before she even had a handful of sprouts.

Best get used to it.

"House," she said, closing her eyes, "may I have a wheelbarrow please?"

When she opened them, at first she didn't see a wheelbarrow. *It's mad at me,* she thought, feeling oddly guilty. The house might be very strange, but it had seemed so eager with the dress, perhaps she had offended it in some fashion.

Then she turned around and there it was, a bright red wheelbarrow.

"Thank you, House," she said, nodding her head toward the manor, where dozens of windows watched her like eyes. "This is perfect." She picked up the handles and grinned involuntarily as her arms dropped into the correct position. "And you have even noticed that I am rather short. That is very kind of you."

"At home," she continued, talking to the house, because there was clearly someone there listening, "at home my wheelbarrow is made for someone taller. My sister Holly can use it just fine, but I am always having to keep my arms crooked up to keep it from dragging, and it's not very comfortable."

She filled two wheelbarrow loads with her plants and pushed them to her corner. Spread out, even with the promise of seeds to come, they seemed very widely spaced. "Well, you'll have plenty of room to grow," she told them. "Tomorrow I will start digging, and perhaps House can find me some mulch."

She peeled her gloves off and stuffed them in her back pocket, patted the wheelbarrow absently, as she would Fumblefoot, and began the long trudge to the house and her room.

On the landing above the stairs, she paused at a lovely celadon urn. It would have been even better with something growing in it—stonecrop, perhaps, or a tumble of pansies—but it was very graceful, and most importantly, not pink.

Hmm.

"House," she said aloud, "this is quite a lovely urn. Would it be okay if I took it to my room?"

She raised her eyes to the ceiling, listening. There were no strange rumbles or heavy silences. Apparently House did not object.

When she lowered her eyes, the urn was gone.

"Oh. Err. I could have moved it myself, but…thank you?"

Bryony went to her room, saw the door opening before she even touched it, and went inside. The urn was now proudly displayed by the window, with a spray of feathery pink grass in it.

Compromise. This is a compromise.

She peeled off her sweaty clothes and laid them across the bed. "Um. House, do you think you could have these cleaned? Do you do that? I'd be grateful." She turned to the basin to lave water over her arms, and when she turned back, the clothes were gone.

I just hope it gives them back afterwards.

House had left a robe hanging by the washstand. There was a tray on the table by the window with a bunch of grapes, some cheese, and a small loaf of bread. Bryony pulled on the robe and investigated the tray.

Well…I suppose I have to eat the food sometime. And it's not like I didn't already eat the bacon and the eggs, and they didn't kill me…

She popped a grape off the stem and ate it.

Nothing horrible happened. It tasted like a grape.

The second one also tasted like a grape, as did the third. The bread was still warm. (Presumably if you were conjuring bread out of thin air, it wasn't much more work to make it taste fresh from the oven.) The cheese was perfectly good cheese.

Bryony made short work of the lunch. Feeling exhausted—*it has already been an extraordinarily long day, and surely it cannot be much past noon*—she lay down on the big pink bed and fell instantly asleep.

When she woke, it was growing dark outside the window.

"Good lord," she said, sitting up, "did I sleep that long? Was I that tired?"

She washed her face in the basin. The water was still warm and perfectly clean, as if invisible maids had been flitting about while she slept.

Perhaps they are. If there are servants here, they are invisible, assuming they're anything so separate as servants, and not…err…tendrils of House.

This was a somewhat uncomfortable mental image.

When she turned, the green-striped dress was arrayed across the bed in all its excessive glory.

Bryony sighed. She had never much liked dressing up in the old days, not like Iris, who would have worn ball-gowns to breakfast given the chance. Still, this was what the house, and presumably the Beast, expected her to wear.

There were underthings hidden under the dress. She pulled them on, glad that they all hooked up the front. She was growing used to House's habit of making things appear, but the thought of having magic hands touch her, even just to lace up a corset or do up a row of buttons, made her skin crawl a little.

She imagined that it would feel like a centipede wiggling over her arm. She hoped that House didn't see her shudder.

It is not wise to hurt the house's feelings.

The dress went on easily enough. She had to do one little sideways shimmy to get a snap fastened at a particular spot on her back, but the old skills came back to her easily. They had had a maid in the capital, but she had spent most of her time either helping Iris or trying to make Holly more presentable and less pink. Bryony had learned to fend for herself.

She put on the bracelets and the horse-collar necklace, but drew the line there. "You'll tear my earlobes off with those things," she said, waving to a pair of emerald earrings the size of a trowel blade, "and I am *not* going to wear a tiara. Tiaras are for princesses and little girls pretending to be princesses. I was a merchant's daughter, not a princess. The only princess I ever met was nearly forty and had a squint."

When she glanced back at the bed, the tiara was gone. The bed had straightened itself, pulling the sheets and blanket tight. The pillows had been plumped. Bryony wondered if she would have actually seen it happen, if she'd been looking.

Is it better to see it happen, or to catch it out of the corner of your eye?

I have no idea. I suppose I'll probably have an opinion in a week or two, though, if House keeps straightening itself when I'm not looking.

There were shoes. They were actually comfortable, which was impressive, since her feet were unfashionably wide and had once been the despair of cobblers. In the last few years, she had taken to wearing men's boots and shoving a wadded up sock in each toe.

Decked out in finery, she left the room and walked to the staircase. The Beast was waiting at the foot.

He was wearing dark green, a kind of open tunic over a robe with large sleeves, but the sash at his waist had a pattern of silver leaves on it.

Bryony the gardener would have stomped down the steps in her usual manner, but Bryony who had once been the daughter of the richest merchant in the land remembered how one descended a staircase. *Fingertips on the bannister, chin up, one hand holding up your gown so that you do not trip over your own clothes and break your neck…*

"You do that very well," said the Beast.

"You never forget some things," said Bryony. Three deportment teachers had nearly broken themselves training those things into her, and one had actually quit and gone into the seminary afterwards.

The Beast offered her his arm.

She took it, because of all those long-lost deportment teachers, even though his nearness made it hard to breathe. She did not have to touch his fur—that would have been too much, too soon—but his sleeve was warm and velvety, almost like fur itself.

The air did not seem to go deep enough into her lungs. He moved slowly, but she still took two steps for every one of his.

He smelled like cloves and fur and something dark and musky. It was the smell of a wild animal, not a tame one.

A door opened before them, and then another, and they came to a dining hall so large that the roof was lost in shadow. There was an enormous table with a linen table cloth and glittering silver, and food was packed onto it on gigantic plates and salvers and steaming tureens.

"Oh dear Lord," said Bryony.

Wrought-iron candlesticks lit the table wherever there was a square inch to spare between dishes. Candlelight gleamed from aspics and sauces, from the curve of apples and grapes and the glistening flank of roasted fowl.

"You don't expect me to eat all this, do you?" she asked the Beast.

He shook his head. "Not at all. The house is—err—extravagant. Eat whatever you wish."

"It won't go to waste, will it?" asked Bryony, eyeing a roasted peacock on a platter the size of a wagon wheel. "I mean…surely some of this is compostable, at least…"

"Nothing will be wasted," said the Beast. He released her arm and pulled a chair out for her at the head of the table. His feet made no sound on the floor, but the chair screeked nicely against the tiles, which made Bryony obscurely pleased. It would not be pleasant to be the only thing in an enchanted house that made any kind of sound.

She sat. The Beast took a chair at the corner beside her.

"Oh, thank goodness. I'd hate for you to sit at the other end, and have to yell over the peacock at you."

The Beast's eyes crinkled up. "That would be inelegant, yes." He reached for a bottle. "Do you drink wine?"

"At this point," said Bryony, "I would drink raw moonshine. It has been a very long day."

"The house can probably provide raw moonshine, although you would offend its sensibilities." The Beast poured out a glass.

Bryony took a sip. It was dry and sweet and seemed to evaporate off her tongue and through the roof of her mouth.

The Beast set the glass down and did not pour out another.

"Do you not drink wine?"

He shrugged. "I do. But I cannot drink it from a glass. I would require a dish to lap it from. It is…unsightly."

"Ah."

A slightly uncomfortable silence fell. Bryony leaned over the table and stabbed a fork into a slice of roasted peacock.

She had made inroads into the peacock, some peculiar salad with a nutty dressing, and a tureen of mashed potatoes when she finally realized that the Beast wasn't eating either.

"You're not eating?"

He shrugged again. "I am a Beast."

"So does that mean you live on what? Air and sunbeams?"

He wrinkled his snout. "It means that I eat like a beast."

She sighed. "And I suppose that's unsightly, too?"

"Very."

"This is going to be a *long* dinner," said Bryony, taking another gulp of wine.

She made it through another slice of peacock before the silence got to be too much for her. "So. Err. Tell me about yourself. How did you get here?"

The Beast opened his mouth and a wind seemed to rush through the hall, snuffing out many of the candles. In the sudden gloom, his shadow rose up on the wall behind him like a giant.

Bryony froze with her hand on the wineglass. A drop of condensation slid down the side and over her fingers, cool as a sigh.

"I cannot say," he said firmly.

Magic. There is definitely some magic here. He doesn't want to talk, or something's stopping him.

Bryony cast about for something else. "What do you do to occupy your time?"

He propped his muzzle up on one enormous paw. "I read a great deal. The library is very large. Sometimes I build things."

"What sort of things?"

"Clockwork, mostly. The house is not good with clocks. The insides confuse it, I think. It makes things that look like clocks, but they run mostly by magic. I tinker with them and try to make them work without magic. Sometimes I make little wind-up things."

Bryony eyed the size of his—hands? paws?—and wondered what qualified as "little" to a Beast. She was pleased to have found a safe topic, however. "What sort of things?"

He scrabbled his hands across the tablecloth. It was hard to read that enormous face, but she thought he was embarrassed. "Nothing much. A ladybug that walked, once. A bird that chimed. Although when I tried to make another ladybug, it didn't work, so the first one is in pieces around the room, until I figure out what went wrong."

Bryony laughed.

By the time she had finished a small slice of pie and pushed her plate away, the candles had re-lit themselves. She stifled a yawn against her fingers. *How can I be tired? I slept all afternoon!*

"Sorry," she said.

The Beast shook his head. "Don't be. You may sleep a great deal for a few days. There is something about magic that takes people that way. It should wear off soon."

"Good to know." She pushed her chair back and stood up.

"Will you marry me?" asked the Beast.

Bryony froze.

"I'm sorry," she said, when she could talk again, "I think I may have misheard you."

"I said 'Will you marry me?'"

She stared at him.

"It's a simple enough question," said the Beast testily. "You can say no if you like. I rather expect you to. I'm not going to kill and eat you if you—are you *laughing?*"

Bryony sank back down in her chair, shaking with hysterical laughter.

It had always been her besetting sin. Here she was in an enchanted castle with a monster and magic at every corner, her father dead and her family's money gone, a sister who was going to have to marry the weaver's son, and *now*, finally, someone offered to marry her?

What she could see of the Beast's expression was so nonplussed that she only laughed harder.

God, she had been the despair of so many lady's maids! All those ridiculous balls and all those poor women trying to make her look presentable in hopes of teasing out an offer of marriage from some scion of a great house. "Now Miss Bryony, stand up straight and don't slouch." All those pumice stones trying to whittle away at her big, bony hands, outsized compared to the rest of her, all those paints and powders trying to make her jaw less square and her nose less beaky. "Now Miss Bryony, don't rub your eyes or you'll smear your makeup!"

All that effort wasted trying to catch the master of a great house, and now that she had no money and no prospects, she had the master of the greatest manor house she had ever seen asking to marry her?

And he can't possibly care that I'm not pretty, because he's some kind of boar-bear-monster thing!

She slid down in the chair and thumped on the arm and didn't stop until her bladder threatened to mutiny.

"Water closet," she gasped, half-crawling out of the chair. A door opened out of the wall. She wasn't sure if there had been a door there before or if House had made one, and she didn't care. She sprinted for it.

When she emerged, trying to settle the ruffled skirt again, the Beast was standing behind his chair.

"Feeling better?" he asked.

"Much," she said. It was true. Something had unknotted while laughing. If she was going to be trapped in an enchanted castle, at least she would be trapped with her sense of humor intact.

"If it is all the same to you, Beast," said Bryony, inclining her head as if she were still that long-ago girl, "I would prefer *not* to marry you."

"I can hardly say that I am surprised," he said dryly. "I did not expect to be laughed at quite so enthusiastically, however."

"Oh, well, that." She waved a hand. "That wasn't at *you*. That was at my father and a great many well-meaning maids and a little bit at myself."

"Then I shall take no offense," said the Beast. "May I escort you to your room?"

"I don't know. Seems rather forward of you, doesn't it?"

One lip curled up in a toothy grin. "The foot of the stairs, then? I should not wish to cause any *talk.*"

"Heaven forbid." She took his arm. Her lungs immediately seemed shallower, but after such a good laugh, she was willing to put up with it as far as the staircase.

When they reached the foot of the stairs, the Beast released her arm and bowed to her. She curtsied—the full skirts made doing so a rather silly pleasure—and ran up the steps.

"Good night, Bryony," called the Beast.

"Good night, Beast," said Bryony.

CHAPTER TWELVE

Bryony woke in the night and knew that there were things outside the window.

She kept her eyes squeezed tightly shut, not wanting to give herself away. With the bed-curtains open, it was only the shadows that concealed her. Her blanket was pulled up over one shoulder. If she rolled over, pretending to still be asleep, could she pull it over her head?

She was aware, even as she thought these things, that she was not being rational. If there were truly things outside her window, and not just childhood monsters hiding in the dark, then a blanket over her head would be no defense at all.

Was there something there? Was this just a night terror?

They're there. They're real. I'm sure of it.

Had it been a sound that had woken her? Something tapping on the glass?

If she opened her eyes and looked to the window, would she see a pale face pressed against it, watching her?

Bryony had spent most of her life jumping into bed to avoid things grabbing her ankles, even when she was supposed to be grown up and well past that stage. A succession of nurses looking under the bed when she was a child hadn't helped. She always pictured some shadowy thing pressed against the underside of the mattress, spread-eagled and thin so that a glance under the bed-skirts did not reveal it.

Later on, when she took her courage in her hands to look herself, she still wasn't quite convinced. Bare floorboards and dust bunnies were all well and good, but perhaps it was listening for her and hiding behind the headboard when she checked. Then when she stood up, it would flow back down under the bed and wait.

It was an old familiar terror, and Bryony was used to it. This, however…this was something else again.

Something was there. Something unknown but real.

Bryony opened her eyes a slit. Dread lay like a knot of roots in her belly.

She dragged her gaze from the bed-curtains to the window. She could barely see and she didn't dare open her eyes any wider.

Something white flashed on the other side of the glass.

It's the birch, it's only the branches, that's why it looks so long and pale and twisty, those aren't fingers, it's only the birch, the birch, only the birch—

Part of her knew that it had to be the birch tree. Another, rather larger part was sure that it wasn't.

I can roll off the bed. I'll roll to the side, and…be at the mercy of whatever is lurking underneath.

Shut up shut up there's nothing under the bed there's never anything under the bed you're not a child why aren't you over this?

Something tapped, very quietly, against the window.

It's only the branches there's nothing there branches tap sometimes…

Could it open the window? Would House let it in?

Was it part of the magic of this place?

Had the Beast, for all his talk, brought her here as a sacrifice for the things outside the window?

There's nothing outside the window. It's only a tree. If you can't open your eyes all the way and look and stop scaring yourself silly, you had better pull the blankets over your head and try to go back to sleep.

Feeling as if she were nine years old again, Bryony burrowed down into the blankets, trying to make it look as if she were asleep and getting comfortable. You couldn't look as if you were awake, that was one of the rules. Monsters couldn't get you while you were asleep.

Indeed, the only monster she knew had gotten her while she was awake, and brought her to live in his enchanted manor house. Maybe there was something to the rules of childhood after all.

She pulled the blanket over her head, leaving a crack between pillow and blanket to breathe through. It was hot and stuffy and uncomfortable, but it was safe.

Happy now?

Well, happier, *anyway…*

She fell asleep like that, still listening for the sound of something at the window.

When she woke the next morning, Bryony did not have any moment where she wondered where she was and what she was doing there. The pinkness of the room was a very efficient reminder.

She hadn't been able to draw the bed-curtains without feeling as if she'd been stuffed back into the womb, but the room was pleasantly warm, even with no fireplace in sight. She peered over the side of the bed, did not see anything—

Like pale white hands reaching out from under the bed?

—and slid her feet down to the floor.

"Well. Still alive," she said to the house. "Didn't get eaten by monsters last night after all." She glanced at the window, at the white tracery of birch branches, and felt foolish.

I suppose the house is judging me now.

Of course, the house can see if I scratch my butt or pick my nose and it can watch me in the water closet if it wants to, so I suppose it was only a matter of time.

She was washing her face when she heard her name spoken aloud.

"*Bryony…*" said a high metallic voice. "*Bryony…Bryony…*"

She froze with the cloth still over her face.

"*…Bryony…Bryony…*"

It's in the room with me. It's in the room and oh God, what if it came from under the bed, what if it was waiting and it's going to grab me what if it's right behind me oh God—

She yanked the cloth away from her eyes and whirled.

There was nothing, and then there was a great deal of pain because the soap had gotten into her eyes.

Bryony cursed and rubbed and blinked and by the time her eyes no longer smarted violently, the voice had stopped.

Had it been a person? A *thing?* What was it? She eyed the room with great suspicion, but there was no one there.

Out loud, she said "Is someone there?"

There was no reply. She suddenly smelled bacon.

It was coming from the little table by the window. Eggs, bacon, a cup of hot tea, toast with jam…

"House, you are *wonderful.*"

She was instantly ravenous. If there was a voice, assuming it hadn't been some fragment of a dream, it didn't appear to be malicious. She sat down at the table and took a bite.

Knowing that the bacon was not, in the strictest sense, *real* did not make it taste any less delicious.

It can't just be an illusion. I was full after dinner last night, and the Beast doesn't seem to have starved to death. I wonder how long he's been living here, eating the food?

She wondered if it was one of those questions that the house didn't seem to like.

Is it the house that doesn't like them? That does that strange listening thing when I ask?

Another thing to watch for. Bryony's questions were starting to pile up.

"House, may I have paper and pen?"

Something rustled. When she turned, an armoire in the corner had folded out to reveal a rosewood writing desk. An extravagantly curled quill pen stood beside several sheets of writing paper.

The feather was pink. So was the paper.

Bryony sighed. *I should probably have expected that.*
She sat down and dipped the pen in the ink.

How long has the Beast been here?
Why doesn't he leave?
Has he always been a Beast?
Where does the magic of the house come from?
What does he want with me?
What was that voice?

She brushed the feather against her cheek and thought for a minute, then added a final question:

How do I get out of here without the house bringing me back?

"Of course," she said aloud, "for all I know, he was lying about that, and I could walk out the front door at any time."

She didn't think he'd been lying.

"Oh well," she said, blowing on the ink to dry it, "I suppose I'll figure it all out eventually. Now, to see about the garden…"

The grass cut easily and there was some lovely topsoil under the sod, but Bryony was still soaked with sweat by the time she came in for lunch. She took a hot bath in a pink enameled tub with dragon feet. The bubbles were pale pink and smelled of freesia.

She added another question to her mental inventory—*What is going on with all of these flowers?* There were the rose candlesticks and the dahlia rug and all the little blossoms embroidered into her clothes, the enormous rosebushes in the courtyard, growing into the bark of the birch tree—

Which is pretty strange, when you think about it.

She liked flowers. She just liked them outside, where they belonged.

Although I should probably do something about those roses and the birch tree. That can't be healthy.

It was a good soak. The bathtub was long enough to stretch out in. She hadn't had a really hot bath since they left the capital. At home, in the cottage, she and her sisters usually filled an old wooden tub in front of the fireplace, and the water was never warm enough.

She leaned her head back. "I could get used to this, House. This is lovely. Thank you."

She took a long nap again that afternoon and woke to find a blue dress laid out on the bed. It was the color of a late evening sky. It would have been magnificent on Iris.

"It's a pity you didn't get my sister," she told the house, trying to manage the little puffed sleeves. "She'd be much more interested in playing dress-up. No, still not wearing the tiara. No, nor the gloves either. I will wear earrings if you can make them smaller than a dinner plate—ah, yes. Perfect."

She checked her appearance in the mirror. The clothing was extremely flattering, but short of a veil, there wasn't much it could do about her face. She grinned ruefully at herself.

"On the other hand, Iris would probably not have stopped weeping yet, and I imagine that would strain even a magic house's patience."

She went down to dinner.

The Beast met her at the foot of the stairs again and escorted her to the hallway in silence.

He poured her a glass of wine without speaking. She stabbed at the food on her plate with a fork, and finally took refuge in the most banal possible conversation.

"Do you think it will rain?"

He leaned back in his chair. "It's hard to tell with spring weather," he said. "It changes too quickly. It could rain all morning and be clear by dinner."

"True," she said. *Well, it's a boring conversation, but better than nothing...* "Sometimes in Lostfarthing, you get a light rain, and then the fog comes up from the ground so thick you can't see your feet."

"I've seen that," he agreed. "Here and—err—elsewhere."

She finished the last of her meal and pushed the plate away. "You said that there's a library in the house. Could you show me where it is?"

"I would be honored," he said, but made no move to rise.

Bryony raised an eyebrow.

"Bryony, will you marry me?" asked the Beast.

"Are we going to do this every night, then?" she asked.

"It seems likely, yes."

She sighed. "No, Beast, I do not want to marry you. You've been a very considerate kidnapper, but I am not quite resigned to my fate yet."

"I should hardly expect you to be." He stood up and pulled out her chair. She had a brief impression that he could have picked up the chair—with her in it—in one hand and tossed it over his shoulder. She rose as gracefully as she could and took his arm.

The Beast's library was as large as the dining hall and had a ceiling that vanished up into shadow. A ladder with wheels attached to it stood ready in case one needed the highest volumes. In the center, lit by oil lamps, stood a semi-circle of shorter bookcases arranged around two large wingback chairs.

"Good heavens," said Bryony. "You have hundreds of books!"

"Thousands," said the Beast. "There is another storeroom besides this one. I cataloged them once or twice, long ago. These are merely the ones I wish to have close to hand. The house cannot create new books—or rather it can, but the insides are gibberish—so I have read all of them, already."

Bryony turned slowly in a circle. Even at a book a day, there were weeks...months...years... Each bookcase seemed to represent decades.

If he's read them all—even if he's a fast reader—that's—dear lord...
She now had at least a partial answer to one of her questions.
The Beast had been here for at least a century.

CHAPTER THIRTEEN

She took several volumes to bed with her. One was of poetry. She hadn't read poetry in years. She hadn't read *anything* in years, and was a little embarrassed at the sheer greed that the Beast's library awoke in her.

As for the notion that the Beast was a great deal older than she had suspected…Well, she didn't quite know what to make of that. There was no grey in his fur. He did not seem particularly arthritic. Perhaps Beasts aged differently than humans.

And will I grow old and die here, in this strange gilded cage, while he remains unchanging?

There was an old, old story she remembered, about brother and sister turned into swans. They had lived for a thousand years as swans, and then a saint had prayed over them and changed them back. For one moment they had been human—and then a thousand years of age caught up with them, and they crumbled into dust.

At that point, you have to question whether being a swan is really that bad…

This line of thought was not terribly helpful.

She tried to lose herself in the novel that she had selected. A young heroine in a strange, possibly haunted house, lots of ghosts and treacherous servants, exactly the sort of thing she had loved in the city.

It did not work quite so well in the Beast's manor. "At least *you* can leave," she told the heroine. "And I'd give a lot for a human servant to talk to, even a treacherous one." She sighed. A few pages later she added "The dear sweet children in distress are clearly the evil masterminds. Idiot." A few pages after that she gave up entirely.

Bryony pulled the bed-curtains closed. It was just about as bad as she expected. They were gauzy enough that she could still make out shapes in the room, as if through a dense pink fog.

House extinguished the candles. She burrowed down into the pillows.

As she fell down the dark well of sleep, a last thought came to her.

What if I'm not the first?

"Bryony….Bryony…Bryony…"

The sound woke her. The horrible voice was back, saying her name, and furthermore *it was right next to her ear.*

Her heart shuddered and leapt. She stared into the pink depths of the bed-curtains, her eyes wide.

If I look over, what am I going to see? Is there going to be something there?

She had a stark vision of hands reaching up from underneath the bed, attached to a terrible creature whispering her name.

"Bryony…Bryony…"

"No!" shrieked Bryony, sitting up in bed. "*Stop!*"

She flung her arm sideways, sweeping aside the curtains, and there, on the nightstand, stood a clock.

Golden nightingales perched atop it. As she watched, they opened their beaks and sang *"Bryony…Bryony…"*

She sagged back on the pillow, feeling damp with relief.

"It's a cuckoo clock. A stupid…horrible…*personalized* cuckoo clock."

She rubbed her hands over her face, feeling like ten kinds of idiot.

The birds said her name a few more times, then closed their beaks. Bryony sighed.

It was odd, though. She was awake much earlier than she had been the night before. Had she slept through the clock, or was it going off at different times?

"House," she said wearily, "please don't…err…please make them stop doing that, all right?"

When she opened her eyes, the clock was still there. The mechanical nightingales looked vaguely reproachful.

Hopefully they would stop singing now. Bryony went to eat breakfast, and then to turn sod.

"The house would probably do that if you asked," said the Beast, coming up behind her in the garden.

"No," said Bryony, sliding one edge of the shovel under a square of sod and ripping it out with a heave. She flipped the sod into the wheelbarrow. Earthworms fled, wiggling, into the dirt.

"Certainly it would," said the Beast.

"I'm sure it would," said Bryony, setting her shovel down. "I don't want it to." She walked to a tray of lemonade being held aloft by a stone dryad statue. (She found most garden statuary insipid, but the lemonade was too good to complain.)

"Why not?"

Bryony drained a glass of lemonade and set it back down. "Because this is my garden. If I let House build it for me—and then what, weed it and mulch it and prune it as well?—it won't be mine. It'll be a thing that the house made for my amusement."

"Hmm," said the Beast. "I understand that, I think."

"Besides," said Bryony, wiping sweat from her forehead, "it's not like I don't have plenty of time."

"There is that," agreed the Beast. He sounded so humble that it irritated Bryony, who preferred him when he was feeling snappish and sardonic.

"If seeing me out here working bothers you, feel free to grab a shovel and help me strip some of this sod," she said.

He stared at her.

"It's easy," she said. "Here. Here's the shovel. I've already cut it into squares. Shove the blade under just under the grass roots and flip it out. Like peeling a really big orange. With a really big butter knife."

"Your gift for metaphor leaves much to be desired," said the Beast, but he took the shovel. It looked like a toy in his hands. One paw engulfed the end of it. He followed her directions and awkwardly tore up a strip of the lawn.

"We're going to need to get you a bigger shovel," she said. "You'll hurt your back."

"I doubt that," said the Beast, moving on to the next square.

"Hunched over like that? Yes, you will."

"I am functionally immortal, you know."

"Good for you. Do you want to be functionally immortal with a bad back?"

He wrinkled his lips back from his teeth. Bryony gazed back, unimpressed. The Beast surrendered the shovel.

"House," said Bryony, tapping the stone dryad on top of the head. "Can you find me a Beast-sized shovel, please?"

The Beast ran a hand over his face and said "This is not what I expected to be doing this morning."

"Did you have other plans? Don't let me keep you." Bryony turned and found the new shovel against the boxwood hedge. It was nearly as tall as she was, and had a blade like a plow. "Good lord!"

The Beast pulled off his tunic and unbuttoned his cuffs. Rolling up his sleeves took awhile, and revealed enormous biceps as thick as Bryony's waist. His fur was dark and sleek, with brown highlights against the black cloth.

Bryony handed over the shovel.

"Are you sure this won't make it less *your* garden?" he asked, draping his tunic over the boxwood hedge.

"It's a risk I'm willing to take. Be nice, and I might even teach you to mulch."

"Oh. Joy." The Beast attacked the sod, taking out three squares for Bryony's one.

With the Beast's help, the ground was clear by noon. Normally Bryony would have tilled down a bit, but the soil revealed was loose and moist and so much the platonic ideal of good soil that she distrusted it immediately.

"Is there something wrong?" asked the Beast. "You are glaring at that dirt most severely."

"Magic dirt," said Bryony grimly. "No dirt is *this* nice. I don't trust it."

"You could ask the house to make it worse, I suppose," said the Beast. "I am not sure what to tell you. I think it is genuine dirt, not anything created, but I am sure the house has—err—fixed it a bit."

"Hmmm." An earthworm poked its nose out of her handful. Surely nothing with earthworms involved could be *too* evil, could it?

And it's not like you have much choice in the matter…

"All right," she said, returning the worm to the ground. "Get the house to make you a trowel, and we'll get these plants in the ground at last."

"Have you any plans after that?" asked the Beast, acquiring a trowel the size of a short sword.

"Lunch, I suppose…"

"For gardening." He gestured with the trowel, flinging bits of dirt over his clothes. "There are other plants here, after all. They could use…err…pruning?"

He looked at her very intently. Bryony paused with her hands full of oregano.

"The boxwoods don't need it. I think they prune themselves."

The Beast's shoulders sagged, and he returned silently to digging.

CHAPTER FOURTEEN

The next morning, she woke up an hour before dawn, because the damnable mechanical nightingales had gone off again.

She flung a pillow at the birds. They continued to sing her name.

She got up, fury overriding her fear of the shadows under the bed, and snatched up the clock. It was surprisingly heavy. She could probably have brained an intruder to death with it.

Bryony stalked to the closet, snatched a dress off the hook, and wrapped it tightly around the clock.

"*Mrrrongghhnyyeee…*" it called plaintively, through the fabric.

She flung the wadded up dress and clock into the far corner of the closet, slammed the door, and went back to bed.

At about half past eight, they went off again.

Next to her ear.

She yanked the curtains aside, and there was the clock, or one exactly like it, with the mechanical birds singing "*Bryony… Bryony…*" with dreadful clockwork smugness.

"Oh, for the love of…" Bryony stomped to the door, pulling her robe tightly around herself. She pushed the door open and yelled "BEAST!" into the hallway.

It was probably her imagination that the clock was sulking on the nightstand.

"Beast! *Beast!* Are you out there?"

Footsteps pounded down the hallway. Bryony was pleased to see that he finally made a sound on the floor, but when he rounded a corner and she realized that he was running on all fours, she took a step back.

"What is it?" cried the Beast. "Are you hurt? What is wrong?"

"Err—nothing really wrong—" she stammered. He stood up in front of her. His clothes were disheveled and there was a wild gleam in his eyes. She took a step back. "I didn't mean to *alarm* you, I just—"

"I heard you calling," said the Beast. He took a step forward. His nostrils flared, as if scenting for something. "I smell no blood on you."

"The house won't stop this awful clock from saying my name," said Bryony meekly.

The Beast blinked at her several times, then huffed loudly. She thought it was a laugh. *"Oh. Is that all?"*

He put a clawed hand on the doorframe, and appeared to give the wallpaper a very stern look.

When Bryony looked at the nightstand, it was completely bare. There was not so much as the shadow of a metal bird on it.

"Thank you," she said faintly. "Um. I really am sorry. I didn't realize you'd come running."

"If you have need of me at any time," said the Beast, "you have only to call my name. If it is within my power to come to you, I will."

He turned away. Bryony shut the door and locked it.

"Sorry, House," she mumbled, feeling as if she'd been fighting with one of her sisters and a grown-up had just appeared to yell at them both.

The house gave her a cold breakfast. Bryony rather felt that she'd deserved that.

She went down to dinner that night warily. She had not seen the Beast all day, and hoped that he was not angry with her about this morning.

"You seem very quiet," she said, as the doors opened before them.

"I should apologize," he said. "This morning—"

"I'm an idiot. I shouldn't have started yelling for you over a silly little thing like that."

"No, no." He made an impatient gesture with his free hand. "I should not have run. Not on all fours like that. Not where you could see me. I am ashamed."

"It was a little unsettling," she admitted. "But you're certainly very fast."

"I am faster running as a Beast than walking as a man," he said bitterly. "I should have remembered myself, but I was afraid that some harm had befallen you."

"I appreciate the thought." She patted his arm. "Please don't worry about it."

I am reassuring a very large monster that has kidnapped me. I just patted his arm without really thinking about it. You can get used to anything. How nice.

"Besides," she said, as he pulled out her chair, "if something bad *had* happened, I would want you to come with all speed, no matter how it looked."

The Beast bowed his head, as if she had laid some kind of geas upon him, and sat down silently across from her. Bryony sighed from the bottom of her toes.

"Bryony," he said, pulling out her chair at the end of the meal. "Will you marry me?"

"No, Beast," she said.

He nodded and they went to the library side by side.

The next few days settled into a routine that was actually rather pleasant, insomuch as being held captive against one's will in a giant enchanted manor house with a somewhat sarcastic Beast could be.

Bryony got up in the morning, ate, and went down to the garden. The Beast was usually either waiting for her or joined her later.

She worked for much of the morning. It went slower than it might have because she was teaching the Beast, who was polite (if not, she suspected, actually that interested in gardening) but tended to make holes three or four times as deep as were actually needed.

"Good lord," she said, when she saw what he had done in the herb wheel, "it's oregano, not an oak tree."

"My apologies." He scuffled dirt back into place, trying to make the oregano look less forlorn.

"It's all right. I wish I'd had you around when I was trying to put in the currant bushes back home. It took Holly and me three days to dig all the holes." Her breath went out in a sigh at the thought.

She missed her sisters a great deal. Some days she worried at their memory like a sore tooth. If one of them were hurt or killed, would she know? Would she ever find out?

I'd know.

I'll get out of here eventually. I will. I'm learning more all the time. The Beast admitted he was functionally immortal. That's got to be important somehow.

Meanwhile, the plants have to go in the ground.

She was aware, on the days when the Beast was not waiting for her, that she missed his company a little. She did not tell him that. It seemed extremely bad form to tell your captor that you were lonely and that he was the closest thing you had to company.

When all her plants were transplanted, she planted seeds. House provided her with cut poles and twine to make trellises for the peas, and by the time those were built, the first little green radish leaves had come up and it was time to thin the seedlings out.

The Beast had apparently learned his lesson, and did not ask why she was planting vegetables, in a house that gave her all the food she needed.

After the morning's gardening, the days went slower. The air seemed clearer in the garden. Once she went into the building, she felt a weight settle on her shoulders.

Nevertheless, she went inside and washed up and ate lunch. She read for a few hours, and took long afternoon naps. Sometimes she took the books out to the garden, and that helped, too.

Every evening, a new gown was laid out for her, and every evening she put it on, because House really didn't ask for much, and went down to dinner.

She never saw the Beast eating, and every night he asked her to marry him.

Bryony wondered sometimes what would happen if she said yes, but she had a bad feeling about it. Leaving aside the fact that she didn't particularly *want* to get married, what if this was the final aspect of the trap? What if saying yes meant that she put herself into the Beast's power completely?

She preferred his company to solitude, but there was no sense being foolish about it.

Besides, she thought, picking at her lunch, *he's…um. A Beast. Even the blacksmith isn't that big. Marrying him might have some… practical difficulties.*

Iris would have turned purple. Holly would have laughed and embarked on a very dirty-minded discussion of what those practical difficulties were likely to entail. Bryony sighed and picked up another novel.

It was in the library, after dinner, that she was most grateful for the Beast's presence.

As long as she had been able to read, she had been prone to read passages aloud to anyone who happened to be in the room. Mostly it had been nurses, maids, and her sisters. Now, it was the Beast.

Bryony would kick off her shoes and flop into one of the chairs, with her legs over one arm and her head on the other, and whenever she encountered a line that made her laugh, she read it out loud to the Beast.

"Ha! Listen to this one—*'I have no particular predilection for tortoises,' said the prince, 'it is only this particular tortoise that I wish to marry.'* Isn't that marvelous?"

The Beast smiled. Bryony knew that he had to have read the book himself, probably several times, but that did not particularly diminish her enjoyment. She would have read it to House if no one else had been available.

"It occurs to me," rumbled the Beast, looking up from his own book, "that that particular volume may be a trifle scandalous for a young lady of good sensibilities."

"It's a good thing I haven't got any then," said Bryony cheerfully. (Indeed, some of the stories were what Iris would have called "a trifle warm" and which would have made Holly grab the volume and pore over them herself.)

"You have plenty," said the Beast, turning the page. "They all simply seem to be pointed in the wrong direction."

Bryony grinned.

Occasionally, she drank a second glass of wine in the evenings, which made her feel rather giddy and amused, and which one night led to her poking the Beast with one bare toe when she thought he wasn't looking up from his book fast enough.

(A week ago, the notion of touching the Beast voluntarily would have made her tremble, but there was something deeply unthreatening about him when he was reading. He had to fold himself into the chair for one thing. For another, he was desperately near-sighted and had to hold the book a few inches past the end of his muzzle when reading. Apparently House could not provide adequate reading glasses.)

He looked at her toe. She waved it threateningly. "You're not listening. This is a great line."

"You're *poking* me," he said mildly.

"You're lucky I don't come over and hit you with a footstool. What can you possibly be reading that has you so engrossed?"

"A treatise on the subject of aetherometrics."

She scowled. "You made that up." She threatened him with the toe.

"No, but I admit it's rather dry compared to yours." He eyed the toe warily. "Are you going to poke me again? Should I read some of mine to you?"

"Is it as funny as mine?"

"Not even remotely, I fear."

Bryony drew her bare foot back to her own chair. "You don't have any treatises on horticulture, do you?"

He considered. "I've got a few on crop rotation. I shall have to fetch them down for you."

"Are they are dry as aeth—either—your book?"

"You might not think so. I would be happy to get them out, if it saves me another savage poking."

Bryony made a rude noise, then giggled. The Beast smiled down into his book.

No, it was not an unpleasant way to spend an evening.

CHAPTER FIFTEEN

There was someone in the room with her when she woke up.

She wasn't sure how she knew, or why it woke her at all, but she came straight up out of sleep without any confusion.

Someone was there.

She lay frozen under the sheets, her fingers fisted in the pillow-case, listening furiously.

There!

A stealthy footstep, then another. Someone was walking across the room.

What shall I do if he opens the bed-curtains?

Her knife lay on the nightstand. She had been wearing it faithfully, although she had no hope of actually drawing it from under one of those ridiculous dinner dresses, and House was apparently treating it like some essential undergarment, because it never vanished the knife away.

Unfortunately the nightstand was at least two armlengths away, owing to the improbable size of the bed, and she'd have to lunge across the pillows, hope that she didn't get tangled in bedding, grab the knife, and then…something. *Wave it in a war-like manner and hope for the best.*

I won't move. Maybe he'll go away. If he opens the curtains, I'll go for the knife. I'll scream for the Beast and go for the knife.

The footsteps passed around the foot of the bed, moving toward the window.

It did not occur to her that it might have been the Beast moving about her room. The Beast's feet were utterly silent. He could have been in and out any number of times and she would never have heard it.

Unspoken even in her thoughts was a growing belief that the Beast would not have been sneaking around her room in the first place.

The intruder scrabbled at the desk by the wall. There was a frustrated sound to it. Paper tore.

Not here, she thought. *I'm not here. I'm a little mouse. A baby bunny. A very quiet thing that hides very quietly and isn't here at all.*

The scrape of the window opening sounded like a crack of thunder. She jumped, and hoped that he hadn't been watching her.

He can't see me. I can't see him. These stupid pink bed-curtains may be saving my life. Does he know I'm here? Does he think I'm asleep?

Wind sighed through the room from the open window, and then—nothing.

Long hours passed without another sound, but Bryony didn't sleep again until dawn light had broken through the window.

The Beast was waiting by the garden. Bryony strode up to him, scowling.

"There was someone in my room last night," she said.

He stared at her as if she had said that she had decided on roasted barn owl for lunch.

"Impossible," he said finally. "Are you sure you didn't dream it?"

"I'm sure," she said. "Look, everybody gets nightmares, sure. This wasn't one. I heard someone walking in my room. And they did this." She held up the pad from her writing desk.

The list of questions on it was still legible, but barely. Gouges had been torn in the paper and the bottle of ink had been upset on the desk, staining half the page.

"The pen's been snapped in half," she said. "House cleaned up the ink bottle, but it left the rest. I don't know if it can't, or if it wanted me to see this."

"It might not have known it was supposed to," said the Beast absently. He was reading the questions, she realized, and flushed. "The house can't read very well. It can make books, but the insides are just a few words repeated over and over. It can read very simple phrases, so far as I can tell, but nothing complex. It probably knew that the ink bottle wasn't supposed to be overturned, but it couldn't have recreated the writing."

He paused, then added, "I am not always certain how much the house understands."

"It understands clothes," said Bryony dryly. "At least, for a value of 'understand'."

The Beast half-smiled at that, but a frown slowly formed over his face, dragging his lips back from his tusks. "I truly do not know what to tell you." He handed the list back to her. Their eyes met as he handed the page over, fiery yellow to murky green, and he nodded, almost imperceptibly.

There was a great deal more to his eyes than the golden predator's gaze she'd seen at first. There were depths there. Humanity. Heat.

Bryony suddenly found it hard to breathe, and took refuge in outrage.

"You said there wasn't a key to the lock!"

"No, I said that I didn't *have* a key to the lock," he said. "That doesn't mean that one doesn't exist, or couldn't be made." He considered. "If *I* wanted to get into your room, I would simply tear the door off the hinges, but I imagine that you would have mentioned that."

"You could knock," she said acidly.

"Well. There's that." He clasped his hands behind his back and began to wander across the grass. "There are, as I see it, three possibilities."

She fell into step beside him, too annoyed to care that her breath caught when she stood too near the Beast. The scent of cloves and fur mixed with sun-warmed grass.

"The first possibility is that you dreamed it," said the Beast.

"I didn't. And anyway, what about the damage to my papers?"

"You may have done it yourself, either for some obscure reason of your own or while sleepwalking."

Bryony gritted her teeth. "Thanks."

"It is only one possibility. The second, of course, is that I am lying to you and I did indeed break into your room and upset your inkwell myself."

Even angry—and fine, admit it, *scared*—Bryony had to admit that the Beast was being fair. She huffed a laugh. "All right. I'll admit that I don't think you did it any more than I did. I wouldn't have heard you. You're too damn quiet."

"Ah," said the Beast, raising a clawed finger, "but perhaps I *meant* you to hear me."

"For some obscure reason of your own?"

"Precisely. You have only my word for anything here, after all. For all you know, I am trying to frighten you or drive you mad."

"For all I know, I froze to death in the woods and I'm dead and this is Hell," said Bryony testily. "Are you the Devil, by any chance?"

The Beast laughed. It didn't have a great deal of humor in it, but it was definitely a laugh, even if there was a bit of a boar's grunt to it. "I'm not, so far as I know."

"You have to tell me if you are. I'm pretty sure that's a rule."

"Do I? Very well. I don't believe I'm the Devil. I can't imagine that he would allow himself to be so inconvenienced by his form as I am by mine."

"Well then, I'll take your word for it." Bryony ran a hand through her hair, aware that it was probably sticking up like a hedgehog. "What's the third possibility?"

"That you are not mad or dreaming, and there was indeed someone in your room."

"All right." Bryony squared her shoulders. "Is there anyone else in the house?"

The Beast shook his head.

"Could someone be there without you knowing? You said that travelers find the house sometimes, when in need. Could someone have gotten in that way?"

The Beast opened his mouth, then closed it again, looking thoughtful. "I had not considered that. I suppose it is possible. I am generally somewhat—aware—of others in the house or on the grounds, but I would not say that it is impossible."

"Could someone get in by magic?" asked Bryony.

"With sufficient magic, one could get in anywhere, I imagine," said the Beast. "But I would expect to notice that, as well." He, too, ran his hands through his mane, until great tufts stuck up. Bryony had an exasperated urge to smooth them back down. Her sister Holly tended to shove her hair under a hat when working, and when she took the hat off, it went wildly in all directions. It always made Bryony's fingers itch.

She tucked her hands firmly under her arms. "Could someone who was here before simply not have left?"

The Beast considered. "It—has been—a long time." She thought he might be about to say something else, but he shook his head and repeated "A long time. No. I do not believe so."

A queer heaviness settled in Bryony's stomach.

I'm not the first.

She looked over at her garden, at the stalks waving bravely in the morning light, at the fuzzy sage leaves and the grey-green spikes of lavender. *What changes did that other person make? Those other people? Are there signs of the Beast's other victims scattered through the house?*

Did one of them plant the rosebushes? Make the dresses? Design that godawful pink bedroom?

Will some future victim find my garden in a hundred years and think that it's just more of House's magic?

She gulped.

When she looked at the Beast again, he was watching her with his deep golden eyes.

"It is hard to know what to say," he said. His eyes bored into hers.

That's a message. He's trying to tell me something, like he did before, at the gate.

It occurred to Bryony suddenly that she did not *want* the Beast to have victims. Not merely because she did not want to be one (although that went without saying), but because—God have mercy—she *liked* the Beast. He was sharp-tongued and sardonic and occasionally abrupt, and if he had been human, she would have liked him very much indeed.

She bit her lip.

It's just that he turned sod for you. You like anybody who'll do garden chores, admit it.

Well. Maybe a little.

"The poetry you have been writing is interesting," said the Beast out loud, gazing somewhere into the middle distance.

"Poetry?" said Bryony blankly. She looked down at the crumpled paper in her hands, with the list of questions scribbled on it.

"Poetry," said the Beast firmly. "I think you have some potential. It still needs work, of course, but I would be interested to see any future efforts."

She did not need his warning glance to get the message. "Oh. Yes. You're very kind." She scowled down at the page. "I'll keep working on it. If anything else occurs to me, I'll let you know."

CHAPTER SIXTEEN

She was in the library that night, bending over a book on crop rotation, which was just as dry as promised, although there was some very interesting stuff about peas, when the Beast came up behind her and said "Bryony—" and Bryony yelped and threw the book over her head at him.

He caught it and peered down at her, bemused. She had lunged partway out of the chair, caught her shoe in her skirt, and was afraid that if she went any farther, she'd tear the petticoats right out of her dress.

Bryony swallowed. "Sorry. I'm still a little jumpy."

"I would never have guessed." He leaned down and offered her his arm. She hooked her elbow around it, and managed to extract her feet from her skirts without falling down.

"Look," she said, when she was finally back in the chair, "do you think you could—I don't know—make some *noise* when you walk? Just a little? You're so big and you walk so quietly."

"Oh," said the Beast, looking abashed. "Um. I could try. It's my feet. There's hairs between the pads, they muffle everything…" He sat down on a footstool, picked up a bare foot and wiggled his toes at her.

Bryony had not previously considered the Beast's feet very closely. She grabbed his ankle. He made a resigned noise but didn't protest.

They had a large central pad, like a wolf or a tiger, and four toes with black pads. Between each toe was, indeed, thick brown fur.

"Four toes?"

"There's a dewclaw in back," said the Beast, almost apologetically.

"Hmmm," said Bryony, attempting to part the fur with her fingers. "I see the problem." She ran her thumb over the paw-pad, which had heavy, creased hide like a dog's. The claws on his feet were black, blunt, and curved. The dewclaw came around like a sickle.

"Do you have to trim this one?"

"Yes. The house produced any number of clippers before we found one that wouldn't break."

"You didn't have it removed as a young Beast?"

"No," said the Beast dryly, "nor were my ears cropped to conform to breed standard. If you're quite though…?"

"Oh! Yes, sorry." Bryony released his foot. The Beast put it down on the floor and twitched his robes back over it.

"At least you don't have a tail to dock," she said. "Or were you born with one of those, too?"

"I was born quite human," said the Beast. "My mother was very kind and would likely have kept me even if I *had* been born a Beast, but fortunately for all, we did not have to find out. In fa—"

He stopped in mid-word. The air in the library had become suddenly heavy, and there were shadows in the corners that were not at all the friendly shadows of shelves and books.

A rustling noise sprang up around them, like dried leaves rattling in an autumn breeze, and the breeze itself struck them a moment later, although it did not touch the pages of Bryony's book or make the candle flames dance.

Bryony reached out blindly and caught the Beast's sleeve. She felt his hand cover hers, as she tried to peer through the deepening darkness. Even the small shadow under the footstool had become as deep and dark as a well.

"I should not have said that," said the Beast. "Forgive me." Bryony was fairly sure that he was not talking to her.

The strange breeze whistled around them twice more, then whispered away. The rustling leaves fell quiet, and the candlelight grew warmer and pushed back the shadows. Bryony looked to the shelf-ladder, and could see the bindings of the books in its shadow, and even make out the titles on the spines.

"What was—" she started to say.

He squeezed her hand, short and sharp, and she fell silent.

The Beast stared down at his clawed hand, where it lay over her small human one. "I will try to make more noise when I walk."

"That would be very kind," said Bryony, returning to the book in her lap. She made a show of turning the pages, but her eyes did not register a word.

So. The Beast had once been human. And someone…or something…did not want him to speak of it.

Interesting.

There was little to do in the garden at the moment. Bryony puttered around for a few minutes, brushing her fingers over various leaves, crushing the leaves and smelling the pungency of lavender and sage.

She could only do this for about ten minutes or risk denuding the garden, so she shoved her hands in her pockets and scowled.

"You have a fierce expression," said the Beast, coming up behind her.

She didn't jump. He had been making an effort to click his claws on the floor inside the house, but there was nothing he could do in the grass. Still, she was getting used to it.

Apparently you could get used to anything.

"Bees," said Bryony.

The Beast looked around. "Really? Where?"

"That's it. There aren't any." She scowled at the brave white flowers on her peas. "No bees means no pollen means no peas. Or beans or squash or zucchini or tomatoes. The root vegetables will be fine, but if they don't set seed, I'll run out eventually and then no more radishes and rutabaga." She scowled at the rutabaga, which were growing with great enthusiasm in this magical garden.

And it's the least they can do, since they're the reason I'm here in the first place.

"I would not expect bees," said the Beast slowly. "Bees are creatures of order and good magic."

Aha! Bryony's mind pounced on that. The rest of Bryony stayed very still, so as not to wake the listening magic.

"We do get flies," said the Beast, "and some beetles. I don't suppose they'll do?"

There was a faint bitterness to the air, a hint that something could be listening very soon. Bryony talked over the top of it, in hopes of throwing whatever-it-was off the scent. "Not the same. I suppose if House makes me a paintbrush, I can walk around dusting pollen between flowers and pretend to be a bee. Though it's not much fun." She scowled again. "Then again, I don't have much else to do."

"Hmmm," rumbled the Beast. "It is possible, actually, that I may be able to help you. Give me a few days…"

He turned, his cloak flaring, and strode across the lawn. His great feet left gouges in the turf. Bryony knew that the marks would be gone by morning.

Now what was that all about?

At dinner that night he was distracted. When Bryony pressed him, he said only "I have an idea, but it may not work, or it may be beyond my skill. I do not want to promise you what I cannot deliver."

When she pushed her chair back from dinner, he took her arm in a perfunctory fashion. "I will escort you to the library. I have my own work to do."

"You didn't ask," said Bryony.

He blinked at her.

"Oh! Bryony, will you marry—"

"It's all right." She patted his sleeve. "I didn't want you to get in trouble, that's all."

He smiled at her, a real genuine smile that reached his eyes, and then went off to his own devices.

CHAPTER SEVENTEEN

Without the Beast around to dig holes—and keep her enter-tained—she spent much of the next morning pacing back and forth.

The manor house was marvelous for that. It took nearly five minutes to go from her garden, through the front of the house to the courtyard, around the birch tree and back out again. The house opened the necessary doors for her. Bryony could always think bet-ter when she was walking, and she felt that she had need of all her mental powers now.

Bees are creatures of good magic. The Beast doesn't expect to see them here.

That means the magic here isn't good.

Well, that was hardly a surprise, now was it? Even if House sometimes seemed kindly, there was clearly something much, much darker at work.

She abandoned that line of thought in favor of another one.

There had been other people here once. Not for a long time, the Beast had said—but they had been here.

That doesn't actually mean that the Beast had other victims. Or guests. I admit that 'victim' doesn't seem to cover what you are anymore. He could have meant his family or servants or anything.

For all you know, his whole family were turned into Beasts and he's the last one alive.

Functionally immortal. Hmm.

It would have been obvious to a much denser person than Bryony that there were things that the Beast did not, or could not, say out loud.

That listening silence. The breeze. Something was watching them and eavesdropping. Something that limited what the Beast would or could say.

It's House. It has to be the house, doesn't it? It can hear us at any time, and he said not to offend it.

Bryony paced around the birch tree twice. The rose bushes exuded a sweet, heavy aroma into the air.

She hated to think that House might be doing something bad. It always seemed so kind. It had given her a really spectacular wheelbarrow full of chicken manure, and she had dug her gloves into it and danced around, whooping, and the Beast had put his muzzle in his hands and stared at her as if she were crazy.

If evil things could create really excellent chicken manure—other than chickens, which were admittedly borderline wicked, most of them—then what hope was there for the world?

She paced some more. Her plants waved at her from the garden.

If the house wasn't evil, then was the Beast?

She shied away from that thought, not wanting to look more closely at it. Surely it couldn't be the Beast. He had seen her list of questions, and he hadn't gotten angry. He'd hinted as broadly as he could that she needed to find the answers.

"Come on," she muttered to herself, as House opened the doors, *"somebody* has to be the bad guy."

Creepy magic house. Giant terrifying monster. It shouldn't be hard to cast one of them as the villain, and yet…and yet…

And neither of them explains why there was someone in my room!

When she reached the courtyard, there was a tray of warm buns and a wedge of crumbly cheese waiting on a little metal table. She wasn't sure if the table and the chairs had been there before. She rather thought not.

It was as good a place to stop as any. She dropped into the chair and applied herself to the cheese.

The courtyard had not changed. The roses grew in the same way as ever, flowering regardless of the season. She wondered if she should bring them some chicken manure. Even enchanted flowering had to wear a plant out.

They didn't seem to need it. If anything, they were even larger and more vigorous than when Bryony had arrived. The canes wrapped tightly around the birch tree, leaving cuts that oozed crystalized sap.

Maybe she should get in there and cut them back.

The thought made her groan. Mere pruning shears were no match for a really entrenched rose. She'd need a hedge clipper and maybe a suit of plate mail.

"I'll start with the shears," she said, putting her chin in her hand. "I can at least get them away from the trunk…"

The roses were sunk deep around the roots of the birch. They were probably stealing the tree's water, but digging them up might disturb those same roots.

Not that I have any hope of digging them up. Rosebushes that size would take a draft horse on a chain to pull out.

Well, whatever the tree needed, it was pretty clear that the *Beast* needed her help.

Help to do what? What if he wasn't the good one?

If she helped him, and it turned out that he was an astonishingly good actor and had been evil all along, and went off to begin eating nuns and small children….well…

"I'll cross that bridge when I come to it," she told the birch tree, and thought she heard the leaves rustling in agreement.

It took two hours to free the birch tree from the roses, and most of that was tying the roses back enough to get in close to the trunk.

The rose thorns were wickedly curved and had a malicious bite to them. When she pulled them out, the wounds throbbed as if they had left venom behind.

Nevertheless, once Bryony had started, she would be damned if she was going to admit defeat. Her gloves were streaked with sap by the time she fought her way to the birch trunk, but at last she could reach out a hand and pat the white bark of the tree.

"There you are," she said, in the same tone she would have used to address Fumblefoot. "There you go. Just let me get these nasty bits out of you…"

The rose whips were embedded so deeply that the trunk had swelled and overgrown them. She had to hack through wood to get at some of them, which her shears were completely unsuited for.

"House?" she said. "May I have a saw?"

A saw did not appear, or if it did, it was somewhere under the roses where she couldn't get to it. Bryony scowled and picked up her shears once more.

It was more butchery than surgery, in the end, but she cut the birch free of the strangling roses. In a few places they had ringed the trunk entirely.

"That might have killed you in another few years," she told the tree. "And then the rose would probably have eaten your stump. Plants can be quite merciless."

She stepped back from her handiwork, down from the raised bed, and onto the tiles of the courtyard.

"Inelegant," she told the tree, "but the roses will grow back and it'll look less awful. Of course, when they grow back, I'll only have to cut them again…"

She went inside, prying a last stubborn bit of thorn out with her teeth. Her clothes were a mass of snagged threads and her shears were dull, but at least she had accomplished something.

When she curled up for a nap that afternoon, she dreamed of a woman in a silver dress, with grey-green eyes. Her face was smooth and youthful, but her voice creaked like an old woman's. She took Bryony's hands, and hers had skin as thin as old parchment, the bones fine and hard within.

"My dear," she said. "Oh, my dear. I think it may be you who will save us. I cannot believe that anyone who is so pleased with chicken manure will be allowed to fail."

Bryony relaxed. There was something odd about the dream—the edges were fuzzier and the woman sharper than any dream she could remember—but if the silver woman understood about chicken manure, then everything would be all right.

"I wish I knew what was going on," she said. "Who *are* you?"

"Someone who was once young and foolish," said the silver woman. "I am old and foolish now, perhaps. There is little that I may tell you, my dear. Be careful." She squeezed Bryony's fingers, like the Beast did when he tried to convey a message. "Be careful of who you trust."

"Can't you tell me anything more specific?" cried Bryony. This was rapidly becoming maddening. This woman looked as if she knew things that Bryony desperately needed to know.

"I am afraid that I cannot."

"Why can't you? What's going on? What is the house? What *was* the Beast? Why is he here? *What does he want from me?*"

She woke up with the last words on her lips, and blew out her breath in frustration.

CHAPTER EIGHTEEN

She was still annoyed at dinner that evening, and took it out by snapping at the Beast. "Another meal where you sit and watch me and I drink wine and try to pretend that there is nothing strange about it?" she growled. "And quit pulling out my chair. I am perfectly capable of sitting down by myself."

The Beast left her chair alone. Bryony flopped down in it. With the skirts, it really was easier with help, which annoyed her even more. She glared at her plate.

"Would you like some wine, or would you prefer to yell at me for a little longer?" asked the Beast pleasantly. "I could leave, if you prefer, but I generally hold that those who leave the room when you wish to yell at them are among the most despicable of beings."

Bryony folded her arms. After a minute she said "Damn you for being reasonable."

"Also despicable," he agreed. "Shall I yell back?"

"What would you yell?"

"An excellent question." He propped his muzzle up on his hand and wrinkled his nose at her, which made Bryony want to laugh. She squelched it, because she wasn't done being annoyed yet. "I can hardly complain that you are a poor houseguest, as you are not here by choice, and you have in fact been quite mannerly about it."

"Thanks," she said dryly. "I do try."

"Mmm. I suppose I could complain that you are not at all forthcoming about your past—"

"Mister Kettle, may I introduce you to Mister Pot?!"

"—well, yes. And since I cannot give you mine, I can hardly expect you to fall over yourself with every detail of your own history."

"Cannot?" she asked, looking up. "Or *will* not?"

"Cannot," he said firmly, meeting her eyes, and went on meeting them while the candles winked out around them, one by one, and the silence fell thickly over the table.

His eyes were very gold. Even over the smell of food and the sharp tang of wine, she could smell cloves and, strangely, roses.

Cannot. He cannot tell me. This—this magic, whatever it is—is watching to make sure he tells me nothing of his past. He is courting the magic, I think, just by telling me that. He knew it would come, and he did it anyway.

What does it cost him, to try to hint these things to me?

Aware only of a desire to make that awful sense of listening go away, she stammered "I—I did not realize that you would want to know. I am not special. I am a gardener and the youngest of three sisters, and my parents are dead. You know all that."

"Indeed," he said. "And I remember the names of your sisters, and that benighted animal that you call a pony—Fumblefoot, wasn't it? That is very little information. Where did you live, before you came to Lostfarthing?"

The candles were beginning to wink on again.

"I came from the capital," said Bryony. The Beast hadn't poured her any wine. She picked up the wine bottle and splashed some out herself. Her hands were shaking a little, which infuriated her.

She had just realized that the silence frightened her. The listening sound seemed to suck at her bones. If it went on long enough, surely it would strip the marrow from them and leave her picked clean on the dining room floor.

The Beast took the bottle away from her and poured out a measured glass.

"You might as well pour yourself one," she said wearily. "Ask the house for a bowl or something."

He stiffened. "It is—"

"Unsightly, I know. Beast, does it matter? You are what you are. I promise that I will not be horrified if you lap your wine instead of sipping it." She rubbed a hand over her eyes. "Perhaps I should beg your pardon for sipping it. Who is to say which one of us is doing it correctly?"

The Beast was silent for a long moment. Then he turned and reached out a hand into the glittering mass of tableware, and drew out a glass.

It looked rather like a brandy snifter that had suffered some middle-age spread. The bowl was broad and shallow. The Beast poured nearly half the bottle of wine into it and then held it to his muzzle and dipped his tongue into it.

It was like watching a bear drink. His tusks were well back and while he made slightly more noise than a human might, he was not nearly as loud as a dog or Fumblefoot.

"You note that I have not screamed in horror," said Bryony, when the Beast had set the glass down on the table. "Frankly, I think you've been exaggerating. I've seen much worse from people who didn't have tusks in the way."

The Beast gave her a hangdog look. She grinned and reached for her own wineglass.

Progress, of a sort. In a few more years, he might even agree to eat at the same table.

She suppressed a sigh at the thought of spending years here. *Surely not. I will get to the bottom of this foolishness and then go back to my sisters. It will not be years. I will not allow it to be years.*

"Why did you leave the capital?" asked the Beast, gazing at her over the rim of his wineglass.

Bryony bit her lip. Having forced him to expose himself, apparently he was going to take payment in kind. Still, she'd started it.

And I can hardly complain that he isn't telling me anything when I'm not telling him anything. Not that any of it matters now anyway, it's all just a stupid and sordid tale.

"My father was a merchant," she said. "Heh. No, I am not being entirely honest. My father was the wealthiest merchant in the city, and he made sure that everyone knew it."

The Beast waited. Bryony grabbed a roll and began buttering it savagely.

"He was good at what he did, but after our mother died, he got reckless. He began gambling on investments that he shouldn't have. Things with ships. I don't know all the details." She waved the butter knife at him.

The Beast smiled. "I was never a banker. I would not know either. Go on."

"Right. Well, in addition to that, he started trying to marry us off. Iris had a lot of offers, but Father was always dead set against marrying anybody who wasn't nobility." She shrugged a shoulder. "He was a commoner, you see, and Mother was some kind of minor noble, a Viscountess once removed or something, and he wanted us to marry someone 'appropriate to our station.'" She glared at the roll and set it down. The Beast refilled her wineglass.

"So there were a lot of very expensive balls and ball-gowns and tutors and whatnot. He might not have had to spend so much on Iris, since she's the pretty one, but Holly and I are…well…" She made a gesture to take in her lack of height and wealth of nose. "Holly's taller than I am, but she also turns pink if she's the slightest bit out of breath, and the fashion at the capital is—was—for pale alabaster maidens, preferably with consumption. And there's never been a fashion for big noses."

"Your nose does not strike *me* as terribly big."

"Are you kidding?" Bryony put a hand up to the offending feature. "And it's crooked, too. I wanted to wear a full face veil everywhere and pretend to be a woman of mystery."

"Compared to mine," said the Beast, gazing down the length of his muzzle, "it is of very little consequence."

Bryony giggled.

I should definitely eat more than a roll before I have any more wine…

"That doesn't work for being short, though," she said. "You're, what, seven feet tall? I'm definitely short next to you."

"My dear Bryony," said the Beast, "*everyone* is short next to me."

"All right, all right. Unfortunately, you weren't one of the available dukes or barons or earls or whatever."

Frankly, I might have thought differently if he were. At least you can have a conversation with the Beast.

"At any rate," she said, helping herself to the food, "it didn't go well. Nobody wanted to be saddled with us, and we brought Iris down with us. I don't know if you know nobles, but having 'a smell of the shop' about you is about like being a cannibal, if not worse."

"I am familiar with nobles," said the Beast grimly.

Bryony waited a moment to see if the candles would go out again, but apparently the magic did not consider this a dangerous statement.

"So there Father was, mounting up huge bills trying to find a fortune-hunter with good enough blood to marry his regrettable daughters, and making riskier and riskier investments, and one day, bam!" She brought her hands together over her plate. "Everything fell down. Our creditors took all of it. I was fourteen."

"Young to be trying to marry you off," said the Beast.

Bryony shrugged. "I don't think anybody expected me to actually be…err…*married* married. Father was hoping to find an impoverished Duke or someone willing to partner me off to an underage son in return for a very large dowry. I would have probably stayed in my father's house until I was sixteen or seventeen." She gazed into her wineglass. "As it was, we loaded ourselves into a wagon—a borrowed wagon at that—and went off to Lostfarthing. There was a cottage there that none of our creditors wanted. My brother—I've got a brother, by the way, for all the good it does—took himself off to the army. He doesn't know where to find us and we don't know how to find him, and good riddance."

That was an uncomfortably raw statement to leave hanging. She swallowed, and added, "And I learned how to garden." She rubbed her thumb along the calluses left by the shovel.

"What about your father?" asked the Beast.

"Dead," said Bryony shortly. "He got word that one of the ships had come back and there'd be some money on it, so nothing would stop him but he should go back to the city and get it. He still had visions of returning us to wealth and glory, you see, even though Holly and I wanted none of it. I suppose it would have been all right for Iris."

The Beast put his muzzle in his hand. "And?"

"Mmm? Oh. Anyway, I suppose he did get some money out of it, because bandits killed him on the way home and took it all." She scowled down at her plate.

"I am sorry," said the Beast.

"Don't be," said Bryony. "He wasn't a very nice man. We were not exactly happy, you understand, but afterwards, there was a kind of relief that we wouldn't have to keep having the same fights over and over again."

The Beast nodded. "I understand that very well. My father and I…" He was silent for a moment. "There are things I wish I could have said, now. But I am also glad that there are things that I did not need to keep saying."

"I used to have long fights with him inside my head," admitted Bryony. "I still do, sometimes. At first I felt bad about it, but Holly said that just because people are dead, they don't become saints, and feeling guilty doesn't make them any less dead."

"I think I would like your sister."

Bryony nodded. "You would. She'd like you, too. You'd get on like a house afire."

The Beast snorted. "I suspect she would be more likely to have me drawn and quartered for making off with you."

126

"Oh." Bryony felt as if she'd slammed into a wall. For a moment, she had almost forgotten that the Beast, regardless of his sympathy, was holding her against her will. "Oh. Well. I suppose."

"Will you marry me, Bryony?"

She lifted the wineglass. "How can I, Beast?" she said, but did not meet his eyes.

CHAPTER NINETEEN

The next morning, he came down to the garden, holding a small wooden box in his hands.

"Here," he said, holding it out. "I made you this. I'm not sure if it will work, but it's worth a try."

Bryony looked at the box, looked up at him, and said "Um…?"

"Open it," he said, barely looking at her, as if he had done something shameful.

She cracked the lid.

Nestled on a black velvet sheet, like a piece of jewelry, was an exquisite bee made of brass and silver.

It was as large as Bryony's thumb. There was a tiny key sticking out of its back.

"Wind it up," said the Beast. "It should go for several hours, but it has to be wound."

Hardly daring to breathe, Bryony wound the tiny key. It took half a minute or more, then it made a sharp *click!* and the bee lifted its wings.

She held the box out, her hand trembling a little, and the bee crawled to the edge. Its legs were fine copper wires, ending in miniature bottle brushes.

"To carry the pollen," the Beast said. "It seemed best not to stray too far from the original design."

The bee spread its wings, vibrated them, and launched itself into the air. Bryony waited, her stomach clenched—surely it must fall! Surely it was too heavy to fly!

It buzzed ponderously through the air, circled the garden, and landed on one of the peas. The bee's golden head vanished into a pink flower, then it pulled back and climbed up the stalk to the next one.

"Flying takes a great deal of energy," said the Beast. "It will walk and climb as much as it can. And it is not as fast as a normal bee, but it is tireless. If you wind it up in the morning—"

Bryony turned and threw her arms around the Beast's neck.

He made a sound of surprise. "I—uh—Bryony—?"

"This is the best thing," said Bryony into his shoulder. "This is the nicest thing anyone has ever done for me. *Thank you*, Beast."

After a moment, his arms came up around her, very cautiously, and they embraced together in the garden, listening to the buzzing of the clockwork bee.

As if her first dream had been a signal, Bryony's nights became far more active than ever before.

It was two nights later that she dreamed of a man, with pale skin and dark red hair, who watched her from across the room. His eyes were as intense as the Beast's, but green instead of gold, a color clearer and less muddied than Bryony's own.

"Who are you?" she asked. "And where am I?"

"You are here," said the green-eyed man, which wasn't helpful at all. When she looked down, she seemed to be in the manor house still. The tiles underfoot looked familiar, and there was a pattern of roses stenciled on the wall. The room smelled of roses too, rich and deep.

"But who are you?"

He smiled. It didn't touch his eyes. When he reached out and took her hand, Bryony felt a jolt go through her, as if she'd been stabbed by a thorn. It was not painful exactly, but she half-expected to see blood.

"I am here," he said, which wasn't exactly an answer. His fingers stroked across the back of her hand. Bryony felt her heart pounding in her ears, and somewhere rather lower than her ears.

Oh, this is going to be one of those dreams, is it?

But it wasn't, and when she woke up, that was almost as frustrating as not having someone to answer her questions.

She dreamed of him the next night, too, and then woke up and stared into the dark reaches of the bed canopy and said "Really? *Really?*"

This gave way to vague nightmares, the sort where no matter how hard to you try, you cannot run from the things pursuing you, but only plod slowly forward, and then to an even more unpleasant series of dreams where she *could* fight back and whatever nameless creatures she was fighting refused to stay dead.

This was hardly restful.

Her afternoon naps got longer and longer because they were the only good sleep that she was getting, and she stayed up later and later in the library with the Beast.

"I am using you shamefully to keep myself from sleeping," she told him. "My dreams are a horror."

The Beast snorted. "I do not mind being so used. If you were not here, you would likely be sleeping perfectly well, and I hold myself accountable."

"Even if it means that I read bad poetry to you aloud?" She lifted the volume in her hands, a work of breathtaking awfulness by a very sincere poet.

"I shall consider it my penance."

"Then brace yourself for *Ode To A Rose Not So Sweet As My Mistress's Voice.*"

"I am ready," said the Beast, and reached for the wine.

She got through three of the poems before she choked up with laughing, halfway through *My Heart Is Trapped Like A Waterbird In The First Ice Of Winter.* "Oh, this poor poet. What's his name—the Honorable Matthias Irving. Oh dear. Poor man."

"There are other volumes of poetry in the library," said the Beast. "Some of them are quite good."

"Never say it." She put her hands over the book's covers. "You'll hurt poor Mister Irving's feelings. Besides, good poetry generally leaves me feeling melancholy and inadequate. But bad poetry is a thing of joy."

"Not precisely the word I would have chosen."

"No, truly. I love this. I do not think I can tell you how much I love this."

"I am beginning to form quite a good idea," said the Beast.

She dreamed of the green-eyed man that night, watching her in a crowd. She recognized some of the people from the capital and tried to get past them, murmuring apologies. When they would not move she became more aggressive, shoving them aside and ignoring the muttering behind her.

She reached him finally, and he said "You have the power to help me. You must help me."

"Maybe," said Bryony, who was suspicious even in dreams. "Help you *what?*"

But he would not say. The crowd pressed in on her, and she woke.

CHAPTER TWENTY

It was a slow grey day, and the garden needed rain worse than it needed her presence. Bryony tried to be grateful that she would not have to water.

Although come to think of it, the soil is so perfectly moist all the time...if I didn't water, would it actually dry out?

She chewed on her lower lip. She had been willing to overlook the magical nature of the chicken manure, but this was treading perilously close to the line. If her plants grew in magic soil, were they hers? Or did they belong to House?

No. It's mine. It has to be mine. Something in this mad place where I am given everything I want—except answers—must be mine. I will not live here like someone's poor relation.

In the end, Bryony went exploring in the house. The thick silence settled around her and she began humming tunelessly as she walked, just to keep it at bay.

There were doors and doors and more doors. She had opened most of the ones by her rooms, but there were whole wings of the house that she had never seen.

She picked one at random, because the pattern on the long carpet runner was an attractive one, and walked down the hall.

The first door she opened was a sitting room, no different from a dozen others in the house. "We could ask how many sitting rooms one manor house needs," said Bryony, "but we wouldn't get an answer, so we won't."

The second door was also a sitting room. So was the third.

"If this is another sitting room, I'm trying another hallway," she announced to the air, and opened another door.

Movement inside caught her eye. She flinched back, startled, and the shadow on the other side of the door flinched as well, and she realized that there was an enormous mirror.

She stepped inside the room. There were mirrors everywhere, reflecting her in an endless ring. Bryony waved her hands and watched the thousand Bryonys wave back.

Underneath the mirrors, at waist height, were low tables. Each table was crammed with jewelry boxes, their lids thrown back, revealing bracelets and necklaces and earrings and rings as plentiful as coins.

"No, thanks," said Bryony, wrinkling her nose. "I get enough of that from House." She trailed her fingers through a jewelry box and felt herself entirely unmoved.

I suppose I could come and play dress-up some cold winter afternoon…or drag the Beast here, to play it with me. She smiled at the thought.

There was a bracelet in front of the largest mirror, made of flat pieces strung together and enameled with a pattern of sharp-edged leaves. House seemed to be fond of it, since it was lying by itself in a little velvet case. "Very pretty," said Bryony, "but not very practical for a gardener."

There was a book lying on one table. She picked it up and opened to the first page.

Haunch of deer, it read. *Deer. Deer. Haunch of deer. Haunch of deer. Deer.*

Bryony blinked.

She turned a few pages, and saw nothing but the same phrase repeated hundreds of times.

Does this mean something? Is it some kind of code?

She flipped halfway through the book and the words changed.

Six yards of linen. Yards of linen. Yards of linen. Six yards. Linen linen. Six yards of linen.

"It's a shopping list," said Bryony, with dawning realization. "Oh, House! You tried to make a book, didn't you, and didn't know how to fill it?"

The Beast had told her that the house could read a little, but that it filled books with gibberish. Here was an example.

She turned pages, discovering chapters devoted to the need for twenty cabbages, a packet of needles, and five lengths of rope.

It should have been funny, but there was something tragic and obsessive about the words written over and over. She turned to the very end.

Out, said the last chapter. *Out out out out out. We are out. Out. Out. Out.*

Bryony set the book down, very carefully, and wiped her hands on her skirts as if she had touched something unpleasant.

It has to mean that it's out of—of cabbages and linen and deer haunches—normal things. That's all. It's a shopping list.

She found that she had no desire to read any more of House's books.

She left the room behind and crossed the hall.

The next room was full of birds.

Bryony froze on the threshold, with her hand still clutching the knob.

There were birds of all shapes, all sizes, all descriptions. There were enormous eagles and tiny hummingbirds, great owls and strutting peacocks. There were partridge and pheasant and robins and ravens. There were birds that she could not name, with huge crests and beaks like shears; birds walking, birds flying, birds roosting with their heads under their wings.

And every single one of them was dead.

"I am not opposed to taxidermy," said Bryony in a high voice, "but this is carrying it a little too far…"

Glass eyes glittered at her. She did not step into the room, but she reached out and touched the wing of a nearby owl. It was soft and still, the same temperature as the air.

She shut the door, very carefully, locking away that silent aviary, and thought that perhaps she was done exploring for the day.

"This house has some *very* strange things in it," she informed the Beast that night, in the library.

"A great truth," said the Beast. "But what in particular?"

She told him about the room full of stuffed birds.

"Oh, that," said the Beast. "Yes. There's one full of beasts, too." He paused. "Well, wild beasts. Not beasts like me, of course."

She had a brief image of a hall full of stuffed Beasts, grimaced, and cast about for a way to change the subject.

"Will you show me how you made the bee?"

He looked surprised, but put his book down. "Of course. Well, I can show you my workshop at least. Now?"

"Is now bad?" She glanced around the library. "I could make an appointment if you like…"

"It's a bit of a mess," he said apologetically. "I'm not in the habit of cleaning my workshop."

She snorted. "When we first met, I wet myself. I think you've still got the social upper hand."

The Beast smirked. "You make a valid point."

They went through three doors, into a hallway that Bryony didn't recognize.

Not that that means anything. I should sit down and try to map this place out sometime, rather than just go through the doors House opens for me.

The fourth door opened into a room smaller than Bryony's bedroom, and unlike every other room in the house so far, this one was a disaster.

"I'm sorry," said the Beast awkwardly. "I can't let the house clean it or I can't find anything afterwards."

Sheets of metal gleamed from every surface. There were three worktables, all of them of a height suited to a seven-foot Beast, strewn with strange tools and dozens of tiny cogs, springs, and gizmos. It looked as if someone had taken a hundred clocks and dropped them on the room from a great height.

"Good heavens," said Bryony. "What is all this?"

"Parts," said the Beast. "I started by taking apart a clock and then I read several books on it. Then I couldn't put the clock back together at first, so I had to read even more books. I started punching my own gears out of metal. I have a very small forge, even, for pulling wires, but I do not use it often. Fur burns very enthusiastically."

A sudden, horrible thought struck Bryony. "You didn't make the nightingale clock, did you?" She put a hand to her mouth. Had she flung the Beast's handiwork into the closet?

He laughed. "No. House made that. I have, I like to think, much better taste than that." The Beast shook his head. "And it wasn't a real clock, either. You said it kept going off at odd hours?"

Bryony nodded.

"House makes things that look like clocks and then enchants them to work. I am not surprised if the timing was peculiar. Whereas I make things that are actually clockwork." He smiled ruefully. "House's creations work, if not always reliably. Mine are reliable, *if* I can make them work at all."

It occurred to Bryony that when she had insisted on making a garden herself, and not letting House do it, that she was following the same path as the Beast in his workshop.

If our every wish is granted, we begin to invent work for ourselves, so that we have a thing that we have earned that is ours...

She felt a sudden rush of kinship for the Beast.

Bryony walked up to a table and stood on tip-toes to peer over it. "But how do you *do* all this?"

"Carefully. I have a great many tools."

She investigated the cleanest of the three tables. This one had something assembled on it. It appeared to be a large brass beetle— no, a ladybug? It looked unfinished. Several legs and a shell casing lay to one side, and part of its back was open, revealing tiny cogs and flywheels.

"I have one that works," said the Beast. "Here, let me wind it up—" He pulled a small bit of brass off a high shelf and set it on the table in front of her.

It was a grasshopper. It was extraordinarily beautiful. Bryony had seen little clockwork toys in the capital, although they were expensive even for merchant's daughters, but this one was larger than any of them. Its body gleamed as golden as the Beast's eyes, and its legs were long and elegant and inlaid with pearl.

The Beast picked up a tool rather like a screwdriver, with a thick handle and a delicate point. He set it in a small recess in the grasshopper's back and began turning it. It made a soft clicking sound as he wound it.

After a moment he removed the tool and stepped back.

The golden grasshopper clicked for a moment, lifted each leg in turn, and then gave a short clattery hop. Bryony jumped, startled, then laughed out loud.

It made another, shorter hop, then slowed. Its legs ratcheted downward and it sank into immobility, poised for another leap.

"The jumping doesn't last long," he said apologetically. "The other ones—the ones that walk—can run a lot longer, but then I usually take them apart for parts because I'm feeling too lazy to make new ones. To make your bee, I had to make finer springs than any I have ever made before, and I wasn't entirely sure it would work."

"These must have taken you forever!"

The Beast lifted one shoulder in a shrug. "I have had much time. And whoever stocked the library in the house had many books on the subject. I believe it was a hobby of theirs."

"So you didn't create the library?"

"No, it was here when House—"

A candle went out. The Beast stopped talking immediately and bent his head over the worktable, moving the ladybug's small gold antennae around in a circle.

The pressure in the room eased.

"These are beautiful," said Bryony. "My bee is the most beautiful of all, but these are wonderful too."

The Beast ducked his head and smiled. If you had told Bryony a month ago that a monster could look sheepish, she would not have believed you. "I am glad you like them. I should concentrate more on finishing them, but it is easy to abandon a project partway through."

"Tell me about it," said Bryony, with feeling. "I've lost plants because I couldn't get it together to dig a hole soon enough." She smiled down at the grasshopper.

"Here," said the Beast, picking up a small volume from the desk. "Speaking of books, and plants, I found this, and thought that it might interest you. It's about gardening."

Bryony took it. The frontispiece said *A Brief Monograph On Flora Of The Northern Forest Regions.* When she opened a page, the writing was very small.

She smiled. "A subtle way of telling me that you are tired of Master Irving's poetry?"

"Not at all," said the Beast. "You may read me anything you wish, at all hours if you like. But I thought you might find it… interesting."

Something about his emphasis on the last word caught her attention. She flipped several pages and halted.

The Beast had underlined something. When she turned another page, there was another underline, and another.

She looked up at him sharply, to find his eyes boring into hers.

Throughout the book, the Beast had underlined two phrases, wherever they appeared.

The first one was, "birch tree."

The second was, "wild rose."

CHAPTER TWENTY-ONE

Her dreams grew worse. She chased the green-eyed man through hallways and faceless crowds. Things chased her in return. Sometimes she wasn't sure who was running and who was seeking, or the dreams blended together without an end.

Once she managed to catch up with him.

"I found you!" she said, breaking out of the crowd.

"You haven't found me yet," he said. His face was sad, but his eyes gleamed. "If you find me—if you *help* me—"

"Help you what?" she asked, half-mad with frustration.

He put a finger over her lips. The touch jolted her, intimate and shocking, and she woke immediately.

Catching him did not seem to help.

The next night, she did not chase him. She turned her back, when she saw him, and pushed her way through the crowd. Was she at a ball? It looked a little like a ball. The people around her wore elaborate clothes, but they faded away when she looked in their faces.

There is always a refreshment table at a ball. I will go find it and I will have a glass of punch. I will not chase anyone.

She was so determined on this course that she reached a wall of the chamber—was it a ballroom? The walls did not seem quite right. She had the feeling that there was something outside the windows, something dangerous.

I will not look through the windows. I will walk along this wall until I get to a corner.

The wall went on for miles, it seemed, and she was pushing her way past dancers in taffeta and lace. Their dresses rustled and brushed against her as if she were walking through leaves.

She looked up and saw the corner of the room. Leaning against it, his face in shadow, was the green-eyed man.

He lifted his hand, almost in salute, and she woke.

The next night she caught up to him easily and walked alongside, not speaking, not wanting the dream to end before she got answers or—well, something.

His eyes flicked to her as they walked through the hallways. The windows were stained glass and she did not want to look too closely at them.

"I can help you," he said. "If you help me."

"Help me how?" she asked.

"We can leave this place," he said. "If you can help me."

"But what do you want me to *do?*" she cried, and woke up speaking the word aloud into the empty room.

During the day she would nap near her garden. (Occasionally, she thought of simply pitching a tent out there, but the notion that she might have no walls between her and whatever might roam the grounds at night was too much to bear.) The hum of the clockwork bee seemed to guard her sleep. She occasionally thought of taking it inside with her, to buzz at night, but she was afraid the metal roses on the candlesticks might confuse the poor creature, or worse yet, the intruder in her room might return, and some terrible fate befall it.

At night, she kept herself awake reading.

The Honorable Matthias Irving became a dear, if imaginary, friend. She pictured him as a tall, gawky man with a mild, hopeful expression, wearing clothes with far too many ruffles. She took to holding conversations with him in her head, the way that she sometimes did with her absent sisters.

"What would you say about this situation, Master Irving?" she asked. "A maiden—well, sort of a maiden—held captive in an enchanted manor—"

"Promising," he replied. "O captive maiden, lily fair, fairer far than flower's flare—"

"Try saying *that* five times fast."

"I'm a poet. I get to do these things."

Bryony was aware, even as she argued poetry with herself, that this was more than a little mad.

I'll be having tea parties for him next. Likely it will all end with me wearing men's clothing and standing on the battlements, proclaiming. I wonder if the Beast will even notice?

Leaving aside the nightmares, inactivity chafed at her. The garden needed nothing beyond the occasional snip of the shears. She had honed every blade and edge of her tools to wicked keenness.

At home she would have been harvesting the second crop of peas and putting in the beets, doing her share of the cooking and fighting back weeds. The old chicken coop needed re-building. She wondered if her sisters had gotten to it, or perhaps they had taken the money she brought them and hired a man to do it.

"Inelegant," said Master Irving, sniffing. "Three lovely maids, *like shining flowers upon the grass, a-thwart with dew!* reduced to building homes for fowl. There's no poetry in it."

"There's not much poetry in chickens. It's mostly eggs and poop," she said, and her imaginary poet clutched his ruffles in horror.

She was, if not grateful, at least relieved when a weed appeared in the garden.

It was not a terribly large weed, a little spike that appeared on the edge of one of the flowerbeds. The stem was dark red and it had tiny fuzzy spines and dark knobs that hadn't yet turned into leaves.

"Huh!" said Bryony. "Where did *you* come from?"

Well, you were halfway hoping for one. Don't be surprised when you get it. Not in this house.

141

She thought about leaving it just to see what would happen, but it was too close to the sage, and something about the shape made her suspicious. It had come up too suddenly.

"You're a runner, aren't you?" she said. "Let's find out…"

She grabbed the weed in her gloved hands and began to tug.

It resisted for a moment, then came up easily, and sure enough, it was not an isolated plant but the end of a long, pale runner. Bryony kept the pressure up, seeing the root zigzag up through the bed, trailing tiny root-hairs.

"Don't you dare break…" she muttered.

She followed the runner to the lawn, still pulling. She expected it to break off in the grass, but it had grown thicker and apparently sturdier. It continued to come up through the grass, leaving a broken line of soil behind it.

"What in the name of God are you doing?" asked the Beast, coming up beside her.

"Don't stop me," said Bryony. "I'm pulling a weed. This is amazing."

He raised an eyebrow. "If you say so…"

There was really no way to explain to a non-gardener the sheer visceral joy of pulling a weed up and getting every last inch. Bryony kept tugging, hand over hand, waiting for it to break.

By the time it finally snapped, she had tracked the runner nearly twenty feet and left a scar in the lawn. She held up the end of the weed like a snake and laughed out loud.

"Well, you've killed it," said the Beast. "Shall we ask the house to cook it for dinner? Or do you mount weeds like trophies over the mantelpiece?"

"I might," said Bryony. "If I were going to, it'd be this one. Look at this thing!" She brandished the end at the Beast.

"Very nice," he said. "Err. Is that the right thing to say about a weed? Very fierce?"

"It'd like to be fierce," she said, examining the bit that had come up. "Teeny little thorns…hell, I think it's a rose!"

142

The Beast went very still.

"Some of the big swamp roses send out runners, but I've never seen one go that far," she said. "I wonder where the main root is…"

"Does it matter?" asked the Beast, his voice suddenly harsh. "Burn it, or throw it away."

She looked up at him, startled.

"I'm sorry?" she said, not sure if she should apologize or get angry. "Was I—oh, Lord! Your roses! Should I have left it?"

The Beast stared at her for a long moment. There was a thin rim of white around his eye, like a horse about to bolt. It was unsettling to see.

She was suddenly aware, as she had not been for weeks, how large the Beast was, and how thin the air around him seemed. Her lungs labored and only force of will kept her from panting.

"No," said the Beast, turning his back. "No. Weeds should be pulled."

He stalked away.

CHAPTER TWENTY-TWO

One night, days of troubled sleep later, she heard the footsteps again.

She was awake instantly, and had time to think, *Goddamnit, I wasn't actually having a nightmare that time, I don't think I was even dreaming yet, why am I awake?* before she recognized the stealthy tread.

Bryony had been keeping her knife under her pillow at night. She inched her hand under her head and clutched the hilt, listening to the footsteps outside the bed-curtains.

It sounded like the intruder was pacing back and forth this time. Bryony lay under the blankets, not daring to move.

She'd rehearsed this in her head while tossing shovels of chicken manure about. When the intruder came back, she would draw her blade, fling the bed-curtains back dramatically, and demand to know who he was and why he was there. She'd point the blade at him and shout. She would be furious and bold.

It appeared in practice that she would do none of those things. *Actually, I think I might pee the bed.*

The footsteps reached the desk, turned, and went back toward the door again. She could hear them rounding the foot of the bed while her heart crashed in her ears.

What if he comes to the head of the bed? What if he tears down the bed-curtains? I can't see anything through them, so he shouldn't be able to see me, but what if he does? Oh God, what do I do?

She bit down hard on her lower lip.

Any thoughts, Master Irving?

Master Irving was apparently hiding somewhere safe. She thought of her sister Holly instead.

Don't panic, obviously. If the curtains come down, stab anything you can reach and start screaming for the Beast.

The vision of the Beast running on all fours, faster than any human, comforted her a little. Wherever he was, if he heard her, he'd come. Hopefully that would be soon enough to staunch the bleeding or keep the intruder from dragging her through the window or *something*.

But the curtains did not come down. The quiet footsteps walked back and forth, from the window to the door, and then finally she heard the sounds of the window being unbolted, and then silence.

What if it's a trap? What if he's standing there, waiting for me to move?

She waited for what seemed like an eternity, all too aware that time was probably moving in a crawl, and what felt like a year might be less than five minutes. At last, when her choices were to move or to go completely mad in the bed and save everyone the trouble, she slid the knife free of its sheath and moved as quietly as possible to the edge of the bed.

Still nothing. No sounds.

She set a foot down on the floor. Her stomach clenched nauseatingly, waiting for something to clutch at her ankle from under the bed.

Nothing.

She got both feet on the floor, took a deep breath, and flew across the room. She fumbled with the lock for three agonizing seconds, then flung the door open—or tried.

The door hit something heavy and only slightly yielding.

Panic clawed at her throat. She slammed her shoulder into the door, forcing it open, screaming something, she had no idea what. The door moved another few inches, and then the pressure was gone and a dark shape filled in the hallway. In the dim moonlight through the windows on the landing, she saw only a looming shadow.

She thrust her knife at it, still screaming, and felt the hilt torn from her hands.

The shape grunted. "Light!" roared a voice.

And there was light. Candles sprang into flame on every wall.

Bryony's throat closed, stopping her in mid-scream.

The Beast stood over her. Far up on his shoulder, looking very small, the hilt of her knife protruded from his flesh.

Bryony gulped. She wanted to burst into tears but crying seemed rather unhelpful, so she didn't.

The Beast held her eyes for a moment, then reached up and wrenched the knife out. She cringed.

"If you are going to stab me," said the Beast, "I would suggest a much bigger knife. This one is…cute."

"My sister gave it to me," said Bryony weakly, because she couldn't think of anything else to say.

"House can doubtless provide you with a larger selection. I would actually suggest a pitchfork instead, given your existing skill with them." He cleaned the knife off on his sleeve and handed it to her. The fur around the wound was growing dark and matted. Bryony stared at it in fascinated horror.

"You were in front of my door," she said stupidly.

"Yes," he said. "I have been sleeping there since you said there was an intruder."

"That's it!" she said, seizing on this. "He's back! That's why I—I thought you must be—I was going to yell for you—"

The Beast's eyes lit dangerously, and he pushed her to one side. "Here? Now?"

"A few minutes ago," she said, as he pulled the door open the rest of the way. "I waited until I heard him go."

"By your leave," said the Beast, and stepped into her room without waiting for an answer. Bryony followed in his wake.

T. Kingfisher

He prowled the length of the room, his nostrils flaring. Bryony retreated to the doorway.

"The room smells like you," he said finally. "If there is someone else here, I cannot smell it. Only you, and roses."

"That's probably the soap," said Bryony, sighing. "Or the pomanders." She wondered what she smelled like.

Probably sweat and chicken manure. "I keep asking the house for lavender or something, but it seems stuck on roses."

"Roses are very important to it," said the Beast.

"And to you," said Bryony, remembering the Beast's fury over his stolen rose.

"Mm. It is different, but this is not the time to discuss it."

"Would you smell it? If there were someone here?" asked Bryony timidly.

The Beast frowned, bringing his tusks into sharp relief. "My sense of smell is less strong than a hound's, and my own blood is muddling my nose. Perhaps not. I cannot swear that there was no one here."

Bryony sat down on the edge of a chest and ran her fingers over an inlaid spray of leaves. "But he couldn't have come past you, could he?"

The Beast shook his head. "There is no chance."

"But I heard him unlock the window," she said. "If he came in through the window, he would have had to lock it again while he was wandering around—and why would he break in it all?"

"Has anything been taken?" asked the Beast.

Bryony huffed a laugh. "How could I tell? The house keeps the place stuffed with knick-knacks and it changes them out practically by the hour." She looked over at the desk. She had not written any more questions down, and the blank stationary was undisturbed.

The Beast frowned. "It would be very strange to have a burglar here."

"Very strange." She ran a hand through her hair, suddenly aware that she was only wearing a thin nightgown and there was a man—or a general approximation of one—in her bedroom. She found the rose-pink robe and pulled it on. The Beast looked politely away.

"You can say that I'm having a nightmare again," she said bitterly. "Or that I'm doing this just to torment you."

The Beast considered. "I do not believe that," he said finally. "You were genuinely frightened."

She looked up, startled. "I might just be a very good actor."

He shook his head. "You smelled frightened. I do not know that one can fake that. And you were screaming."

"Was I? I suppose I was. But that could mean anything," said Bryony. She didn't know why she was playing her own devil's advocate. Perhaps she merely wanted to hear him say that he trusted her.

The Beast shook his head. "Don't you remember? When you threw the door open, you were screaming for me."

Their eyes met for entirely too long, and Bryony had to look away. "Come on," she said, too abruptly, "I stabbed you, so the least I can do is clean it up."

"It's nothing," said the Beast.

"I stabbed you. With a knife."

"Not very well," he said, almost apologetically. "I fear that it is very shallow."

"Nevertheless, I am going to feel horribly guilty about it unless you let me at least put a bandage on it," she said.

"Oh, well, in that case…" He looked around for somewhere to sit, eyed the bed for a moment, then settled for dropping to his haunches on the carpet.

This put them at about eye-level. "House, some bandages and hot water, please." Bryony studied the Beast's shoulder, and tried to remember what Holly had done the time that Fumblefoot got a string of catbriar wrapped around his hock. "And some small scissors."

The Beast looked faintly alarmed.

"Don't worry, I never stab anyone twice in the same hour. I don't want them to think I'm unoriginal."

"I confess, I am more afraid you will clip me bald."

"Vain Beast." She found the tray by the basin, which House had provided with hot water and, of its own volition, a bottle of sharp-smelling astringent. "Can I put this on the wound?"

"If you must," said the Beast.

She soaked a cloth in hot water and wiped at the wound. The Beast gazed over her head with a long-suffering expression.

It took her several minutes with the scissors to trim the hair away from the gash, and the Beast was right, it really was quite shallow. Bryony eyed her handiwork gloomily.

"It's not that I want you to be hurt," she said, "and I'm glad I mostly missed, but still, it doesn't fill me with confidence if I have to stab someone who deserves it."

"I'm sure you'll do better next time," said the Beast encouragingly. "Practice makes perfect."

"Ha ha." She glared at his shoulder. "You've got some hair stuck in the wound. It's going to get nasty if I don't clean it out."

"Do what you have to do."

She had to lean across his arm to get at the shoulder. His fur was short and soft, but there was no give to the muscle at all, a skin of velvet over stone. Bryony snorted.

"Hmmm?"

"You feel like somebody put flocking on a rock."

He laughed at that. She could feel the rumbling against her skin and through the soles of her feet. It was a queer, shivery sensation, not entirely unpleasant, and it made her thoughts go a bit sideways, so she slapped his shoulder the way she would Fumblefoot's. "Quit twitching!"

"Quit making me laugh."

"Hmph!"

His skin shivered like a horse's when she put the astringent on, but he didn't say anything. Bryony was conscious of a sudden desire to rub her thumb over his fur and feel it against her fingers, and crushed it ruthlessly.

She decided against the bandage. It would probably tear out more of the Beast's fur than it would protect the wound. He stood up and bowed to her, very formally.

She fiddled with the washcloth in her hands. "Are you, um, going to keep sleeping in front of my door?"

"I will not, if it makes you uncomfortable."

"Um." She thought about that—about knowing that things were out there in the dark, and about knowing that one of those things would be close at hand if he heard her scream. "No. I don't mind. But if you're going to sleep there, then at least let me get you a pillow."

He laughed again, quietly, as she pulled several of the pillows off the bed. "I would hate to take your pillows."

"I have plenty. Dozens. House must have denuded an entire race of geese to stuff them all." She pushed the pillows into his hands. They looked much smaller when he was carrying them, so she stacked a few more on top. "Do you need blankets, too?"

"No, I beg of you. Fur is very warm."

"Oh. Okay."

At the doorway he paused and looked back, with his arms full of pillows.

"Thank you, Bryony."

"Thank *you*, Beast."

CHAPTER TWENTY-THREE

"How could you?" asked the green-eyed man, stalking away from her down the hallway. Bryony hurried to catch up with him. "I have asked you to help me, over and over—" His voice shook with emotion.

"You have?" Bryony could only remember the one time. "Err. Why are you so angry?"

"You have to help me," said the green-eyed man. "I need your help, and instead you turn to him, my greatest enemy—"

"Who? Slow down!" Bryony caught at his sleeve and felt that familiar jolt go through her. "Who are you talking about? The Beast? Is the Beast your enemy?"

"Why won't you help me?" he demanded, shaking her hand off and stalking through a doorway.

"I *want* to help you," she said. "But I don't know what you want me to do!"

He stopped in front of a window. The lines of his back were eloquent of anger, but as Bryony watched, he slumped.

"No. You don't, do you?"

She joined him at the window. She could not see anything through it except leaves pressed against the glass—a thicket of rose stems.

He turned to her and took her hand. His thumb moved over the back, a tiny caress that made her shiver so hard she thought her teeth would chatter.

"Look at you," he murmured, half-scornfully. "Poor thing. So desperate to be touched that you find yourself half-longing for a Beast."

Bryony felt herself flushing furiously. She hadn't, not really, not *seriously*. It didn't mean anything.

"I should have realized," he said, while she floundered. "Poor thing."

She didn't much like being called 'poor thing,' but then he turned her hand over and stroked his fingers up her wrist. The sensation was so intense that she thought she might drown.

If he touches me again, if he kisses me, I think I'll drop dead.

"You'll help me, won't you?"

"I—" She couldn't think. A place inside her ached. Whether it was her heart or someplace a bit more venal was open to debate.

He took her face in his hands. His fingertips were hard against the hinge of her jaw, almost painful. Her skin felt feverishly sensitive. He stroked his thumb across her cheekbone and she parted her lips and panted like an animal.

She felt desperately ashamed, and moreso when he smiled.

"I knew you would," he said, and bent down and kissed her.

She woke in sheets drenched with sweat and tangled tightly around her feet, shaking uncontrollably.

"Whoa," she said out loud. "Whoa." Her body ached with unfilled desire. There wasn't a damn thing she could do about it, either. Not with the house watching. There were limits. And not with the Beast right outside the door, either, just a few feet away…

She shoved that thought firmly aside.

This is perfectly normal. Perfectly, totally normal. You're just healthy and human and been living like a nun for months. That's all this is.

You'd think if that was all it was, one of these damn dreams could actually go all the way to the end.

"Ungh," she muttered, getting out of bed. The pounding in her head was turning rapidly from lust into a splitting headache.

"Whoa. God's teeth." She stumbled to the basin and splashed tepid water on her face.

In the mirror, her lips looks swollen.

"Biting them in my sleep," she muttered. "That's all it is." She winced. "House, can you find me some headache powders?"

Hot tea and cold water revived her. Her headache subsided and was replaced with an unfocused frustration. She pulled on her clothes and stomped for the door.

"House, have a pile of mulch and a pitchfork waiting for me. A big pile."

The Beast had left, apparently earlier in the morning, leaving a neat stack of pillows by the door. When she reached the garden and found a pile of mulch taller than her head, her temper subsided somewhat.

The garden helped a little. She wasn't sure how long she had been here—a few weeks? A month? The plants had grown furiously. Tall spikes of sage were already hinting at purple flowers to come, and the lamb's ears had unfurled new leaves. The oregano had grown so enthusiastically over its section of the herb wheel that she had to tear up a few of the more aggressive bits, before it ate the basil and began eyeing the lemon verbena. The clockwork bee crawled up the stem of a pole bean, stopping at every creamy flower.

And, irony of ironies, the rutabagas were still flourishing. If they kept this up, she'd have enough to stock a root cellar. Assuming the house had such a thing, or could create one to humor her.

"Maybe I'll dig a root cellar," she said. "That might be a good project to start next. It'd keep me busy, anyway."

And when winter hits, what will I do? Take up meddling with clockwork, like the Beast? Try to find another hobby that the house can't do for me?

Oh, she understood very well why he tinkered with bits of metal and wire, even though House could create magical monstrosities like the nightingales. It would be the only way to keep from going mad.

"I suppose I'll take up hybridizing plants eventually," she said to herself, or possibly Master Irving. She leaned on her pitchfork. "Planting all the seeds and hoping they throw interesting sports. I'll invent my own line of rutabagas."

"*When my mistress among the rutabaga treads…*" said Master Irving, and scowled. "No, it is inelegant. You should have planted primroses. Or bluebells."

"Primroses reseed like the devil," muttered Bryony aloud. *And I am dreaming of terribly attractive men and daydreaming about fussy poets and living in an enchanted manor house with an equally enchanted beast. For the first time in my adult life, weeds are the least of my worries.*

Even if the lawn did not have a single weed in it, she'd brought enough of her own, tucked away in the edges of pots, to make mulch a necessity.

I suppose I could just leave them. I wonder if the sorrel and the goosegrass would eat the lawn, given a chance?

She was too much of a gardener to court such a thing, but she definitely thought about it.

Bryony had slung enough mulch to take the edge off when the Beast arrived. "I should apologize," he said.

"Don't," she said. "I was in no temper for company earlier anyway." She stabbed the fork into the pile again and hefted it onto the nearest flowerbed.

"Not that," he said. He scuffed at the ground with one foot. "I don't think I made it clear enough that I believe there was someone in your room. That you are not mad."

Bryony laughed, not with much humor. "Well, that's something. No, perhaps you're right. Perhaps I'm dreaming it all."

"Dreams in this house are not always false," he said.

She looked up, startled. She could feel a flush rising in her cheeks—did he know?

Don't be stupid. He can't know about your dreams.

Why can't he? The dreams know about him.

They stood on the lawn, looking at each other, with a pitchfork between them. She didn't know whether to laugh or fall down in despair.

"How's the shoulder?" she asked finally.

"Not bad. I heal quickly. It is one of the advantages of being a Beast."

Along with walking silently and being able to smell people. I suppose that's something. I wish I knew how he became a Beast in the first place, but I suppose if I knew that, I'd have half the key to the mystery in my hands. I wish there was some way he could tell me.

Unless…

"I don't suppose you can write, er, 'poetry' yourself," she said, kicking herself for not having thought of it earlier.

If I could just write him a list of questions, and he could write down the answers…

He looked puzzled for a moment, then said "Oh! Ah. No." He paused, clearly picking his words carefully. "I am not good at reading poetry aloud, as you know."

"You're afraid of criticism," said Bryony helpfully.

He looked relieved. "Yes! It has a very…err…silencing effect on one's poetry."

"Oh, indeed. I've noticed." *Are we getting somewhere? I think we're getting somewhere.*

"Those critics have also destroyed my—my confidence in my ability to write poetry in any form," he said, gathering speed. "Which is a shame, because there is nothing I would like so much as to compose an ode to you, believe me."

Bryony laughed, despite her disappointment. "And what would you compose the ode to, Beast?"

"Your questioning nature," he said, and grinned as broadly as Bryony had ever seen.

Metaphor. House is not good at metaphor, or at written things.

He said House could read simple things. I wonder if it read my list of questions, and that's why it dumped ink on them…perhaps he's afraid that it will read anything he writes.

She remembered the fake book she had tried to read—a few phrases repeated hundreds of times. Did House understand the words it had written?

The Beast gave me that other book, though, where he had underlined things…then again, it was a very dense book. Most people in Lostfarthing wouldn't be able to read that. If I hadn't grown up as a merchant's daughter, I would have given up on the first page.

Can I write something complicated enough that House won't understand it?

She toyed with the idea and dismissed it. *Probably not. My vocabulary's not* that *impressive.*

The Beast was looking at her expectantly.

That leaves metaphor. Perhaps we can work around the edges of this…

She moved more mulch with the pitchfork, trying to think of ways to couch her questions.

"It is a shame that you have allowed your critics to silence you," she said finally, smoothing the woodchips around the edges of the lavender.

"Believe me," he said, sitting down in the grass and watching her, "it was not by my own choice. It is a powerful thing, literary criticism. Although I will admit that some of it was perhaps deserved, at least at first. I was a fairly poor poet in my youth."

Interesting. Hmm. I wonder… "And when you were a youth, what sort of poetry did you favor?" she asked. *That should be safe enough. I hope.*

He thought about this for a bit. "The usual sorts. Poems about the joys of hunting in autumn. Dirty limericks. Unrequited love gone bad. That sort of thing."

I can probably dismiss the bit about dirty limericks, and I'm not sure about the hunting. Unrequited love gone bad, though…hmm. Bryony filed that away mentally for later.

"And over time, your tastes changed, I suppose?"

"Quite abruptly, actually."

"Well, it happens that way sometimes."

"Not like this, it doesn't."

Bryony had to fight back a laugh. "I have often found that the worst critics are the ones in your home," she said.

The Beast looked up. She felt the air thicken almost imperceptibly, and hurried to amend her statement. "My sister Holly always laughed at my poetry. She said I made the worst rhymes. If a word didn't have any, I would make up words that would rhyme, like "porrange" and "wilver.""

The sun came out from behind a cloud, and the dangerous moment seemed to pass.

"You are definitely correct about that," said the Beast. "Although I cannot countenance a word like "porrange.""

"Yes, well…"

He agrees that the worst critics are in your home. Does that mean the house, or does he mean that someone close to him did this to him? Oh, damn, I wish this were more precise!

"Still," she said, stabbing her pitchfork tines down and sitting down on the bench, "I love my sister, even if she is my worst critic."

The Beast turned his head toward her, so that she could see his large, inhuman profile. "Perhaps that's the difference," he said. "I never learned to love my critics. Indeed, that was part of the problem."

CHAPTER TWENTY-FOUR

In the library that night, Bryony read another few passages of mediocre poetry aloud, wracking her brain for ways to ask about the Beast's transformation that would not upset the house.

It had occurred to her that she might be making the green-eyed man very angry, but she shoved the thought aside. She was trying to gain information, damnit. And who was he to say what she did? He was a dream. The Beast was real. She couldn't very well avoid the Beast, living in his manor house, and who would say that she even wanted to?

"Oh dear," she said, flipping a page, "poor Master Irving's titles get worse and worse...*Sonnet Written Upon The Death Of A Blacksmith's Child.*"

The Beast snorted into his book.

"But," said Bryony, sliding him a look under her eyelashes, "I should not complain. I have often thought that poetry critics were quite inhuman."

The Beast's eyes flicked up and met hers for an instant.

"Quite inhuman," he said. "Although I expect they look human enough. Before they start to criticize your poetry."

Bryony wanted to crow with delight.

They weren't human! Whoever changed the Beast wasn't human! And he met them as a young man, possibly while hunting in autumn or reciting dirty limericks, and they looked human and...

She got bogged down a bit there, but it was more than she had known yesterday.

"It is a shame that there is no way to silence such critics," she said.

"Oh, there might be," said the Beast. "Yes, I think there definitely might be." He put his book down and looked at her thoughtfully. "Are you avoiding sleeping?"

"Maybe a little," she admitted. "If I'm not in my bedroom, they can't wake me up wandering around it."

The Beast nodded. "Wait here, then," he said, and padded off into the darkness.

Bryony settled back into her chair. The library did not trouble her the way that her bedroom did at night. There were too many books, and books were everyone's friends.

When he returned, he was carrying a pack of cards and two odd little contraptions that looked like very fine tongs with enormous handles.

There was a small table between their chairs. He pulled it up between them (it obliged by becoming larger) and laid out the cards.

"You will have to deal," he said. "It is difficult for me to do. But I can hold the cards with these."

Bryony was fascinated. One set of tongs had broad, flat ends, which held the cards, and the other a small round end that could pick the cards up neatly, while he curled his massive paws around the handles. "Those are amazing!" she said. "Did the house make them?"

"Somewhat," he said. "The first few, at any rate. I have made a number of these over the years, so that I may do finer and more controlled work." He raised a hand, with its blunt nails. "These are not the hands of a watchmaker, so I make do."

"I am quite impressed." She smiled over the deck of cards. "And now I plan to destroy you utterly at cards, Beast."

"You have already failed to do so with a knife," he said, and battle was joined.

The green-eyed man was very angry with her that night. He was still very handsome, and his touch felt like a whip of fire across her skin, but Bryony decided that there were limits to what even dream men could get away with.

"I don't know why you're angry," she said. "And since you won't tell me what I'm supposed to do to help you, you can stay angry, for all I care."

"Would it truly mean so little to you?" he asked, sliding a hand along her arm, waking fire under it. "Just to help me. That's all I ask. Then we could be together outside of dreams."

"I *want* to help you," snapped Bryony, feeling herself shaking, "but you won't tell me what I'm supposed to do!"

He turned away from her and stalked down the hallway. There were windows lining it, throwing bars of moonlight across the carpet. It gleamed blue on his hair and skin when he passed them, a fey, wild look.

Bryony wanted to run after him, throw herself at his feet, probably panting. She didn't, mostly because she could hear Holly in her head saying "Huh! Who died and made *him* the Queen?" and she started laughing.

Her laughter seemed to make a clear space in the thick air of the hallway, but outside that space, things reacted badly. The darkness grew much more intense, until the moonlit windows were pools of light in unbroken shadow. The green-eyed man was gone.

Something touched her back. Bryony leaped forward and saw only blackness behind her, but blackness with something in it. She began to run.

She was aware even as she ran that she was still laughing, that her besetting sin had followed her even into dreams. Even terrified, she still laughed, to keep from screaming.

The pools of moonlight began to wink out, one by one, behind her.

"No more," she growled, waking up. Much more of this would drive her completely barking mad.

She pulled the blankets back and sat up in bed. Her head ached.

Someone was walking toward the bed.

"Enough!" Bryony yelled, suddenly furious beyond measure. She was sick of men in her dreams, sick of the Beast's enforced silences, and most especially she was sick of footsteps coming through her room at night and scaring her senseless.

What if there was someone there? What if whatever-it-was attacked her or hurt her or killed her?

I don't care! I don't care if he uses my entrails to knit baby booties! I HAVE HAD ENOUGH!

She grabbed for the knife and swept the bed-curtains back. "All right, coward!" she yelled. "Show yourself!"

It was dark in the room. There was only moonlight through the window. Bryony looked around wildly, searching for a black shape that might indicate an intruder.

The Beast must have heard her yelling. The door let out two muffled *cracks!* and then he tore it quite neatly off its hinges.

"Light!" he bellowed, and the candles sprang guiltily into flame.

The room was empty.

The window stood open.

"Courtyard!" snapped Bryony. "He was just here! He can't have gone far!"

The Beast nodded and swept her up in one arm, which rather startled Bryony. He tore through the doorway and down the hall, down the stairs at a breakneck pace—certainly faster than Bryony herself would have dared to run—and burst out the door into the courtyard. House barely had time to fling the door open before them, or else she expected that the Beast would simply have torn it off its hinges too.

The courtyard stood silently, bathed in moonlight. Bryony had been avoiding it since the Beast had shown her the book with the words *birch tree* and *wild rose* underlined, wondering if there was something sinister at work there. (The version of Holly in her head had pointed out that perhaps she was *supposed* to go there and begin tearing up the paving or something, but Holly wasn't the one who had to deal with House.)

Now the courtyard looked little different than it had before—except for dozens of white shapes scattered about the ground like giant leaves.

She jerked back in the Beast's arms, and he set her down. "What are those?" she whispered.

"Light!" growled the Beast again, and a candle began to burn on the little iron table. The Beast gave it a contemptuous look and said "*Light*," with a hint of a roar in it.

Lanterns sprang to life above them, and suddenly the courtyard was lit like a festival pavilion. Bryony reached down and picked up one of the white objects.

It was a page from a book. She read the title on it three times before it sank in.

Ode To A Rose Not So Fair As My Mistress's Voice...

"Good God," she said blankly, "someone killed Irving's poetry."

There was absolutely no reason that she should feel like someone had died. It was a book of poems. The Honorable Matthias Irving himself had been dead for several centuries.

They weren't even *good* poems.

Bryony told herself this three or four times and then the Beast picked up the covers, which had been wrenched apart and now hung connected by a dangling thread at the spine. She burst into tears.

"This is stupid," she sobbed. The Beast was holding her, very cautiously, and she was aware that she was making an ungodly mess of his clothes. "I'm sorry. It's only a book. I'm sorry." Saying this made her cry even harder.

"Bryony," said the Beast helplessly. "I'm sorry. It's all right. You can cry for any reason you want." He patted her awkwardly on the back, and she snuffled into his waistcoat.

Get yourself under control. It's just a book. It wasn't a person. You're being stupid.

She took a few deep breaths, trying to choke back the sobs, and was only partly successful. It wasn't logical and it didn't make any sense, but she felt as if someone had taken the Irving she'd been talking to her in head and gutted him.

I'm going mad. Really. This has got to be how it starts. No more. I have got to figure out what's happening. No more napping, no more puttering in the garden, no more card games. I have got to get to the bottom of this, while I've still got a shred of my mind left.

She pushed back from the Beast and ran a hand through her hair. "There wasn't anyone there."

The Beast shook his head.

"I wouldn't have done this," she said. She forced herself to look at the courtyard. Many of the pages were wedged into the rose bushes and impaled on the thorns. "I couldn't have done this."

"No," said the Beast, "you could not have. I do not believe anyone human could—not without looking like a pincushion." He eyed the rosebushes, and his lips pulled back in a snarl.

Wild rose. The rose. The rose is at the bottom of all of this.

I have got to find out how.

CHAPTER TWENTY-FIVE

She dragged herself downstairs the next morning, feeling as if she'd been beaten by hammers.

"You look terrible," said the Beast, who was standing next to the front door, under the protection of the porch.

"Yeah, well, look who's talking." Bryony peered out into the yard and discovered that it was raining, a hard, steady thrumming rain. "Ungh. Well, I suppose we needed it."

"Dreams?" he asked.

"Not after I woke you up." Her door had been repaired in the morning. She hoped that Irving's pages were gone from the courtyard. She didn't think she could face them right now.

The Beast stared out at the rain. After a moment he said, "I hope that you know if you wish to talk about them—about anything—"

"Heh." She dropped her forehead against his arm and slumped against him, resigned. Crying on him the night before seemed to have broken some barrier of intimacy. If she touched him now, what of it? At least she wasn't getting snot on his waistcoat again.

"That's the problem, isn't it? We can't talk about just *anything*, can we?"

The Beast sighed. It occurred to her vaguely that she had been able to breathe normally around the Beast for quite some time now. She wondered when that had happened.

"I suppose not," he said. "I wish we could."

Bryony sighed and pulled herself away. He had been very warm and the air was cold, and she wished that he would put an arm around her, and some other part of her mind said *Have you gone*

164

completely mad? and the part that sounded like Holly said *Oh shut up, what do you know?* and now she was arguing with herself in her head, and if that wasn't madness, what was?

"I miss my sisters," she said.

The Beast nodded. "I'm sorry," he said. "It's my fault."

"Yeah."

She left him on the porch to do whatever melancholy things that Beasts do in the rain, and went pacing through the manor. House obliged by opening doors in front of her, so she walked, more or less at random. She was never quite sure if she was in a hall she knew or another one like it, because they all had the same color carpet and the same candlesticks and not much in the way of artwork.

Her last remarks with the Beast galled her. She could not abide self-pity, but he hadn't seemed particularly self-pitying. Acknowledgement of fault wasn't self-pity, was it?

Does it matter? I should be thinking about getting out of this magical madhouse, not picking at the Beast's motives.

Her thoughts veered much too easily to the Beast. He had held her in the courtyard and he had been enormous and his embrace more solid than any she'd ever experienced.

Was it?

Well, certainly more so than the wainwright's son... Bryony smiled, half-ruefully. The wainwright's son had cheerfully freed her of the burden of virginity last year. It had been a bit messy, a trifle uncomfortable, neither terrible nor amazing. He had, it seemed, mostly been made of elbows and knees. He had gone off to apprentice to his uncle not long after, and Bryony hadn't felt much of a pang on seeing him go.

The Beast was not made of elbows. Presumably he had the usual number. She had never paid close attention. They were probably slightly furry.

I shall have to look the next time his arms are bare. If I can get past all the muscles.

When he had picked her up and run through the house, she had been surprised, but not frightened. No, she was angry and frightened about the intruder in the house, and it had not occurred to her to be frightened of the Beast.

It has been a long time since I have been entirely frightened of the Beast.

She stared at her own feet, not really watching where she was going, glancing up occasionally to the next open door.

Am I asking him the wrong questions? How can I ask what questions I should ask, while phrasing it all in the language of poetry criticism?

She tried to lay out the thoughts in her head as clearly as she could.

The Beast was a young man, and something transformed him. Possibly out of unrequited love, something about hunting and limericks. I don't think that bit's important.

Whatever it was, it wasn't human.

What was it?

"They," she said aloud, stopping and staring at a marble-topped table that had done nothing to merit her intense interest. "*They*. He said 'they.' Not 'it.'"

Was there more than one?

Unless he had been careless with his language. Unless he was being deliberately imprecise to try and throw the house off the track. Of course, sometimes the house felt like two different creatures as well—one of them eager to please, as hopeful as a puppy, one of them listening jealously and throwing tantrums when the Beast came too close to speaking.

She had the nagging feeling that she was on to something here, that she was right at the edge of piecing the mystery together, but she couldn't make it all come into focus. She kept thinking of the rose, *wild rose* underlined in a book, roses twining around the birch tree, the rose on the breakfast table, the single rose that had cost her her freedom.

166

What had he said, all those weeks ago? *You cannot take the rose? The rose cannot leave here.*

Something like that.

Why the rose? Did they catch him with an enchanted rose? And what about the birch tree?

Did he come here once, and grab an enchanted rose?

Bryony paused.

If I stay here too long, will I become a Beast?

Could he have brought me here to take his place?

No, she couldn't believe that. When she first arrived, perhaps she might have, but she had spent too long with the Beast, long enough to hear his sarcasm give way to kindness. Long enough to see him sleeping outside her doorway.

Long enough that she had forgotten that his face was strange, and now it was simply what he looked like. And she was no longer afraid.

She wished Holly were here. Her homesickness had become part of the background now, a thing that she woke up with and went to bed with, a chronic ache she hardly noticed any more. But she wanted Holly here, right now, to say something clever and cutting, to take the pieces that were in her mind and whirl them together and set them down in a pattern that made everything come together.

"What do I do about the Beast?" she asked her absent sister, feeling aggravated tears in her eyes.

You could always jump his bones, suggested her sister. *I probably would have by now.*

"Holly!" Bryony was actually a little shocked, and then started laughing at herself for having conversations with someone who wasn't there and being appalled at what they said.

And here I am roaming the halls and muttering to myself, just like a crazy person again. Oh, how will this all end? Will I go completely mad after all? I suppose the Beast won't have to lock me up in the attic, since I can hardly wander off the grounds by myself...

Another door opened in front of her, and she stepped through it without looking—and froze.

It was another bedroom, much like her own. This one was in white, white sheets, white carpet, white walls, and everywhere white roses.

"Oh," she said, feeling as if she were trespassing, although she knew that no one was there.

Well, the white's not so overwhelming as the pink, although it's a very cold sort of room. Not much color to warm it up. There's a little bit of pink in the roses, I suppose, and the rug there has those burgundy petals, but...

And she stopped then, because it occurred to her that the red-black petals on the rug were not so regular as rose petals, but dark, ugly blotches. She lifted her head, and saw that there were blotches across the sheets as well, and even if Bryony was not so intelligent as her sister, she knew bloodstains perfectly well when she saw them.

The Beast arrived before she was even remotely done screaming.

CHAPTER TWENTY-SIX

She huddled in a parlor, like the one she'd found on the first day, with her teeth chattering and a cup of tea in her hand. She could not seem to stop shaking. House had made tea, which was very sensible of House, wasn't it, the sort of thing Iris might do, not that Iris was sensible, not at all, but she understood tea and that counted for a lot in this world—

"I'm sorry," said the Beast.

Bryony's laughter sounded horrible through her chattering teeth, so she tried to stop it, and when that didn't work, she took a large swallow of tea and tried not to choke.

After a moment she said "So I wasn't the first."

"I never said you were," said the Beast.

There was no reason that she should feel like she'd been kicked in the stomach, none at all. Hadn't she suspected as much? Hadn't she asked herself that question?

Good God, there was blood all over that room, somebody had died there, and she was feeling jealous?

Oh, yes, very sane, very sensible of you. There's another woman! Never mind that she's dead, what bearing could that possibly have on the matter?

"Did you kill her?" asked Bryony. She thought that came out very calmly, considering.

The Beast flinched, as he had not flinched when she stabbed him. He said "No."

Even knowing that he might be lying, relief went shuddering down her spine. Surely there was a logical explanation. Logical explanations were good.

He didn't deny that it was a she, though. Of course, with that bedroom, what else could it be? I doubt House would make a man live in a room covered in roses. There aren't even roses on the Beast's waistcoat, and that changes nearly every day.

It was coppery leaves today, on a black background. She stared at it, because if she had to meet the Beast's eyes, she was going to cry again.

I don't have any reason to cry. I'm not dead, unlike some people.

She took another slug of tea and wondered if she could ask House to put some brandy in it.

"What happened?" she asked.

"I heard you screaming," said the Beast. "I'm sorry, I had to carry you here."

"Not my finest hour," she said. Her voice was quavering, which made her angry. "But yes, I remember that perfectly well." Her face had been pressed against the Beast's chest, and she had wanted to howl like a baby and sob into him and have it all go away, while simultaneously wanting to pull her knife and stab him a couple of dozen times.

Interestingly, neither of those feelings had subsided very much.

"That wasn't what I meant," she said. "What happened—why—"

Why is there a bloody bedroom in your enchanted manor house? Where did she go? What happened? Is that going to happen to me? What is going on?

There were too many questions. The Beast nodded as if she'd managed to actually ask them, instead of stammer herself into silence.

"She killed herself," he said. "Her father took a rose from my table, and I was young and foolish and still thought that I might find a way around the curse."

The candles began to wink out, one by one. The house was listening. The Beast reached out and took one in his hand.

"I demanded that he bring his daughter to me, and he did. I thought she might be able to break the curse."

The air was as thick as syrup. Bryony took a shuddering breath and nearly choked on it. The walls seemed to lean in over them, the ceiling lost in shadow.

It's only the parlor room, they're only walls, they have that stupid rose-pattern border, it can't do anything to us, they're only walls—

Bryony found that she did not believe herself, and stopped trying.

"She did badly," said the Beast. "I think the spirit of the—the—" The horrible silence seemed to slash at him. He hunched his shoulders and retreated from whatever he was going to say. "I think the house tormented her, a little, but mostly it was fear of me. She screamed whenever I came in the room. I would have released her—you must believe me, I would have—but I could not get near her. In order to tell her she was free to go, I would have had to stalk her like an animal through the halls, and I thought that it might drive her mad at last."

The only candle left in the room was the one in the Beast's hand. Candlewax flowed down its sides and over his fingers. It must have burned, even through his fur, but he did not release it.

If he does, it will go out, and we'll be left with whatever's in the dark. She willed him to hold the candle. Her own fingers seemed to be frozen on the handle of the teacup.

"I left her notes, telling her she was free. I do not think she found them."

Of course not. House would have dealt with notes easily, even if it did not know what they said.

"In the end, she committed suicide," said the Beast. "I was too late to stop her. It was so long ago. I thought the house would have cleaned up the blood. I have never seen that room since that day."

The candle was half-burned down now. Bryony had her mouth open and was panting shallowly, trying to get enough air. The room was very hot. She should not be shivering so much when the room was so hot.

"I tried to get word to her father," said the Beast. "When the house took in a traveler, I would leave notes for them, too. I had to hope that they would find him and tell him...something." He shook his head slowly, fur rippling. "And years passed, and when anyone who might have known her would be dead of old age, I stopped trying."

It has been longer than I guessed, Bryony thought. *I do not know what else I would have done in his place.* She wondered if any of the travelers had ever been allowed to see the Beast's notes.

"I should never have kept you here," said the Beast. The candle-light painted orange highlights under his eyes. A human would have looked more villainous, but there was little that mere candle-light could do to his face. "It was a great crime. But when you took the rose—I thought that it was trying to get out—and then you seemed so brave and so fierce, and I had lost all hope, and I thought that you might have the knowledge—I am sorry!"

She heard the apology. On some level she understood it, both the enormous inadequacy of it and the truth behind it. But something else he had said was growing in her mind, something far more important.

"You could have let her go," she said, forcing each word out through the clotted air.

"Yes," he said.

"You could let *me* go," said Bryony.

"Yes," he said.

The room exploded.

CHAPTER TWENTY-SEVEN

The Beast threw himself over Bryony, knocking her back on the couch, so she saw only a flash of light as the candle flared up and then things were flying through the air. The Beast's body shielded hers from the worst of the impacts, but one leg was free and she hissed as debris struck it.

Teacup and I don't know what is and ah! God! that had to be a candlestick, oh God, I think it's throwing chairs at us—

The Beast grunted. She could feel him jerking as furniture struck them. The house was apparently reducing the room to matchsticks.

God's teeth, if this is what happens when you keep talking, I see why the Beast always stopped.

The wind howled. She could hear doors slamming. It appeared that House was having a full-on tantrum.

"Enough," she could hear the Beast saying, although she felt it more than heard it. The word seemed to thrum from his chest through the whole of her body. "Enough. I'm done. I've stopped. Enough."

After what seemed an eternity, the noises stopped. A long time later, the Beast sat up.

Most of the furniture in the room was destroyed. The couch they'd been sitting on was more or less intact, but one arm had been ripped off and hung at a crazy angle. The tapestry over the fireplace was askew, and the fireplace logs were all over the room.

Bryony, feeling slightly squashed, rolled up her trousers and examined her leg.

"Are you hurt?" asked the Beast. "Did it hurt you?"

"Bruises, that's all." She rolled it back down. "Think I took a candlestick to the shin. But what about you? I felt some of those hit."

"It is nothing," said the Beast impatiently.

"The hell it is!" said Bryony. She wasn't sure if she was angry or furious or overjoyed—that she could leave, that they weren't dead, that she believed the Beast when he said he hadn't killed the woman in the white bedroom. Whatever emotion it was, it was near to overflowing.

"You're shaking," said the Beast.

"Never mind that! What happened to you?"

She got her hand on his shoulder and shoved it down. He sat, probably out of politeness. When she stalked around behind him, she could see that his robes had been shredded.

"House," she said, "I need hot water and cloths. And astringent."

When she looked around, nothing had appeared.

"*House.*" She snapped her fingers, as if the building were an unruly dog.

A tray appeared on the floor. It was probably her imagination that it seemed very grudging.

The Beast's fur had protected him from most of the smaller debris, but there were still large splinters jutting out of his back. She pulled them out with her fingers. "So that's why you can't say anything important."

"Yes," said the Beast.

She could feel the house watching them. It seemed sullen but exhausted, as if it had spent its rage.

"And if you tried to say something more than that—"

"It would be worse."

"I see." She pulled the last splinter out and picked up the cloth. They were both silent while she washed the wounds. His shoulders were hunched as if expecting a blow.

I thought that it was trying to get out.

174

What did that mean? What was *it*?

Is he talking about House? Oh God, I can't even ask him out loud!

When she finished, the cloth was pink and stained. She rested her forehead on his shoulder. She could hear him breathing.

His heartbeat was as slow and regular as a clock. Her own had slowed, but it was nothing like steady.

House had tried to physically hurt them. Could easily have killed them.

She had allowed herself to become complacent. It had been so easy. The frilly dresses, the tea trays, the ridiculous roses on everything...

She had forgotten, for a little while, that she was inside an enormous self-aware prison. And apparently it could choose to destroy them at any time.

But perhaps the prison door was open after all.

"Beast," she said, "you have to let me go."

"I know," said the Beast.

He rose to his feet. "Come to my workshop," he said, holding out his hand. "Please."

She nodded.

They walked together through the halls of the house. His feet made no sound, and she was not sure that hers did either. She leaned against him, feeling exhausted beyond measure, feeling as if she had failed.

There is a mystery here. I've known it all along. I knew it the first day. And all this time, and I am no closer to getting to the bottom of it.

And now I'm leaving.

She wondered what Holly would say. Perhaps soon she'd have a chance to ask.

The doors opened for them slowly and shut with a wicked snap behind them. House was still angry. It didn't matter. The long walk to the Beast's workshop, leaning against each other, felt like a retreat from a lost campaign.

I've failed. We didn't win. But now at least I can go home.

When they reached the workshop, the Beast caught the door in his hand and held it for her. He lit an oil lamp himself.

The air seemed clearer than it did in the hallway, untouched by the house's wrath. The light gleamed off all the tiny brass cogs and scattered tools.

The brass ladybug lay on the table. It was much closer to completion than it had been the last time she saw it. One metallic wing lay extended across the worktable, revealing the clockwork inside.

"Here," said the Beast, reaching into a drawer and thrusting his hand toward her, not meeting her eyes. "This is for you."

It was a ring. Bryony peered at it, puzzled. It was made of silver, or some silvery metal, set with a small green stone and a single gear. On one of the teeth, fine as the point of a needle, was etched a tiny leaf.

There was no obvious power source, but as she watched, the gear turned a single notch. The click was almost inaudible. The leaf, which had been pointing at the green stone, now pointed slightly above it.

"If you care to return," said the Beast, "you must do so before it turns completely. When it has completed a full circuit, it will be too late."

"And if I don't care to return?" she asked.

The Beast looked away. "Then throw it away," he said. "I expect you to."

Bryony slid the ring onto her finger. "How do I return?" she asked. "Do I mount up Fumblefoot and ride into the woods and hope?"

She had startled him, she could tell. He took a deep breath. "I'd suggest you come back with fire and an army and burn this place down, but perhaps that's not practical. So hold the ring. Say, "I want to go back to my Beast again." That's all."

"Sounds like something Irving would have written," she said.

A little of the old Beast she knew crept back into his eyes and his voice. "If Irving had written it, it would have rhymed and involved bluebells."

Bryony smiled.

"You should finish the ladybug," she said.

He nodded. "Perhaps I will."

The Beast stood up. He loomed over her in the shadows of the workshop, but she was unafraid.

"Go home, love," he said. "And if you can, forget that any of this ever happened."

He bent down and kissed her on the forehead.

CHAPTER TWENTY-EIGHT

There was a fairy tale that Bryony had read as a child, and most of it she had forgotten. One part of it stuck with her, however, a description of a long and terrible journey—*sometimes she sank, sometimes she swam, sometimes she flew through the air, sometimes she crawled on the ground.*

The journey from the Beast's manor was a little like that.

She could see nothing before her or around her, and she could only sometimes feel the ground under her feet. She thought that she walked forward, but perhaps that was only an illusion.

I do not know if I am flying through the air, but then again, I am not a princess, like the girl in the story was. Perhaps flying is only for princesses. I would feel better if I could see where I was.

She was cold and then she was hot. *Perhaps I am feverish. Perhaps I have been feverish for a long time, and I have only dreamed about a Beast and a manor and a terrible wild rose.*

The silver ring on her finger was cold and hard and she could feel the tiny notches of the gear.

It seemed that things brushed at her as she travelled, things like leaves or branches, and she raised her hands to bat them aside. *Not being able to see is a problem.*

Are my eyes closed? Let's see if—ah, yes. That's better.

There was light ahead of her, fractured into bits. She walked toward it, batting aside the leaves. Definitely they were leaves now, and that was sunlight and…

"Oof!"

Bryony looked down and discovered that she had walked into a split rail fence.

It was such a normal homely thing, to eyes that had become accustomed to marvels, that she wanted to throw her arms around it and weep.

She didn't, because crying on fences was definitely crossing a line somewhere.

It was the fence around the cottage. She climbed over it and into her garden, her own beloved garden, the first one she'd ever planted, with all the mistakes and failures and unexpected glories of a first garden. She loved her new little garden in the corner of the Beast's manor, but this was her heart.

"Oh dear," she said aloud. It was late afternoon. Half the day had passed, somehow, and the sun was starting to sink. "Oh, garden, did you miss me? I missed you. I see that Holly has done her best, but no one ever thins beets enough on the first try, do they? And oregano, you are growing positively out of control, and I do not think that is at all appropriate conditions for a perfectly nice bunch of lupines, and—tell me that isn't mint! *In the ground?*"

It was nearly dark by the time she had grubbed all the mint out to her own satisfaction. (A misleading phrase, really. She would have been much more satisfied if she could have scorched the ground with fire and salt.) She washed her hands in the rain barrel and walked into the cottage, drying them off on her trouser legs.

Holly stood at the kitchen table, chopping up a sausage with a very large knife. She looked thinner and not terribly pleased. Perhaps it was a substandard sausage.

"Gont?" she said, turning toward the door. "Is there something—OH MY GOD!"

She let out a shriek and charged at Bryony, her arms wide, which would have been much more welcoming if not for the butcher knife.

What is with the women in my family running at people with knives? I shall have to ask Iris if she ever does it...

"Put down the knife!" Bryony squeaked, diving behind a chair. "I will hug you as much as you like, but don't stab me!"

Holly flung the knife in the general direction of the sausage and pounced. The next few minutes were a whirl of sobbing and laughing and "Tell me what happened!" and "It's been months!"

Eventually they settled down a bit and Holly poured them both out a glass of cider. "Now tell me," she said. "Tell me everything."

"You first," said Bryony. "Where is Iris? How have you been? I worried about you both so much, but I tried not to—"

"You worried about your garden," said Holly, sniffing. "Which is just fine, let me tell you!"

"Yes, I know, I was out there earlier. You planted the mint in the ground. *Never* plant mint in the ground."

"It's a *plant*. Plants go in the ground."

"Not this one."

Holly made an impatient gesture. "I might have known you'd want to talk plants. Enough! Iris is fine. She moped about for a month and then the weaver's son married her. She still lights a candle for you every night and goes to church and prays long extravagant prayers "for our dear lost one." It's pretty nauseating."

"I'm sorry she's so unhappy," said Bryony, frowning.

"Feh! You don't know our Iris at all, then, or you've forgotten. She loves being miserable. It's her hobby. She'll be a bit put out that you've actually returned, and she'll have to get a new sorrow to milk."

Bryony put a hand over her mouth.

"And did you marry your blacksmith?"

"Gont? Not yet. I may, but he'll have to build me a house. I love his mother dearly, and I will *not* live in the same house with her. Fortunately she feels much the same way."

She leaned forward. "Now. That's all that's happened here. Talk."

"Did you put compost on the garden?"

"I will get the knife if you don't start talking."

Bryony leaned back and exhaled. "Well. Um. I don't know where to start…"

"The beginning. Then the middle. Then the end. Now talk, and I'll try not to interrupt."

In the end she told Holly everything.

She almost left out the bit with the green-eyed man and the frustratingly erotic dreams, but she included them anyway, because they seemed important. The Beast had said that dreams in the house were sometimes true, and she trusted his judgment in the matter.

On her finger, the tiny gear ticked quietly.

Her sister leaned back, when she finally finished, and exhaled slowly.

"I know," said Bryony. "I made a hash of it, didn't I?"

"I love you," said Holly. "You're my sister, and I will always love you. There is absolutely no shame in escaping from a kidnapper, and if you had gutted the Beast and walked out of the house, I would not blame you in the slightest."

Bryony made a faint noise of protest and her sister waved her into silence.

"That said… *God*, you're dumb."

"Very," said Bryony mournfully. "I kept thinking that if you were there, you could figure it all out."

Holly shrugged one shoulder. "I wouldn't say that. I don't know who this fellow in your dreams was, although I'll say I don't much care for the sound of him. But for the love of little green apples, why didn't you just hand the Beast a book and have him start underlining words to spell out his story? You were halfway there with the birch tree thing."

Bryony put her head in her hands.

"The house could read, sort of," she said. "At least, very simple things…"

"Then you could have written up all the possible scenarios in as complicated a form as possible and handed him a list and asked him which poem he liked best. You might have narrowed it down nicely that way."

"In the future," Bryony said, her voice somewhat muffled, "I shall make sure that you are the one kidnapped by magic beasts."

"Oh no," said Holly. "I'm quite comfortable with my black-smith, thank you very much. I've not the least interest in your Beast, except insomuch as he makes you happy."

Bryony lifted her hands and stared at her. Holly shook her head.

"Didn't figure that out for yourself, either? Really?"

"It's a pity we didn't have mail," said Bryony grimly. "You could have sorted all this out for me, and I would have been home in time for tea."

"Quite likely. The solution to the Beast's problem looks bloody obvious to me."

"What? Tell me!"

Holly folded her arms. "The Beast only ever asked you for one thing."

Bryony looked at her blankly.

"I imagine you stopped noticing pretty quickly," said her sister, shaking her head. "You probably got in a routine and stopped paying attention. You do that, you know."

"I am a horrible terrible person," said Bryony. "I freely acknowledge this." She rubbed her thumb over the clockwork ring, feeling the tiny teeth of the gear against her finger. "Now for God's sake, tell me!"

"You didn't say you'd marry him," said Holly gently.

Bryony stared at her. Against her skin, she felt the gear move a notch.

"I'm an idiot," she whispered.

"That's what I said."

"No, no, wait." Bryony clutched at her head. "What if it was more magic? What if I said yes and he *died* or something? I didn't know what it would do! Maybe *I'd* die or the house would eat me or—or—"

"Is the Beast particularly stupid, do you think?" asked Holly.

"No! He's smart! And—and—he's funny. Like we are. Sarcastic. And he makes the most beautiful little clockwork things and he doesn't mind when I poke him and read bad poetry to him and he helped me dig my garden—"

"Spare me the catalog of virtues, I beg of you." Holly lifted her hands. "I haven't forgiven him for kidnapping you yet, although I see that I may shortly be forced to accept him into the family. Don't give me that look. At any rate, if he is *not* stupid, and he had the option *not* to kidnap various travellers, why would he seize only on someone young and female and able to marry him?"

Bryony blinked a few times.

"Now, being me, I'd say nefarious reasons, but since I don't think you're quite so far gone as to be in love with anyone truly evil….well. Marry the monster and be done with it." She scowled. "If it turns out that he is evil, I retain the right to round up a mob of villagers and have him killed."

"I suppose that's fair," said Bryony weakly. "Am I in love with him? Are you sure?"

Holly gazed into her cider. "I believe I need something stronger."

"But—"

"You never get to poke him and read bad poetry at him again," said Holly shortly. "How do you feel?"

A chasm seemed to open up inside Bryony's chest, and her heart and stomach fell into it.

She stood up so fast that the chair pitched over backward. "I have to go back!"

"Well, obviously." Holly picked up the chair. "Settle down. Iris needs to know you're home, and I'll tell Gont where we're going—"

Bryony blinked at her.

"You think I'm letting my baby sister—who has obviously addled her brains with mulch and poetry—go haring off by herself *again?* I don't think so."

Bryony felt a grin spread itself unwillingly across her face. "I can't wait for you to meet him. You'll say such horrible things to each other. I'm sure you'll be friends."

"Right." Holly picked up their mugs. Bryony rubbed a thumb over her ring and looked down at it fondly.

The tiny leaf was a single notch from the green stone.

"Oh shit," said Bryony. "Oh *shit*. Oh—Holly! It's almost done! I have to go back right now! It's moving! Shit! I thought I'd have more time!"

Holly said something that would have sent Iris into a dead faint and dropped both mugs. She swept up the butcher knife in her hand, grabbed Bryony around the waist and said "Just had to spend an hour saying hello to the garden, didn't you? Go!"

The gear tried to move. Bryony shoved her thumb down on it, felt the metal catch on her skin. Over the pinprick of pain, she shouted *"IwanttogobacktomyBeastagain!"*

The world turned inside out.

CHAPTER TWENTY-NINE

If her earlier journey had been vague and feverish, this one was fast and brutal. She would have liked to black out, but that didn't seem to be an option.

A wind tore at them, a wind that howled like a mad dog, and the light of the cottage went red and bloody, shot with black. Then the cottage was gone—had they been blown through the wall?—and Bryony felt her skin being flayed. The wind was beating her with whips of thorns. Holly was still holding her, but even as she recognized the pressure at her waist, it was torn away, and she was alone with the terrible red wind.

I may arrive at the manor house, but I'm not sure I'll be in one piece when I do. Oh God, why didn't the Beast warn me it would feel like this?

Maybe he didn't know.

This seemed likely. She thought perhaps something was trying to bar her way back to the manor, and one magic was pulling her forward and the other was trying to keep her away.

I suppose if one were dragged backward through a thorn bush, while it was on fire, it would be a little like this.

The wind stopped.

She lay in red-shot darkness. She tried to open her eyes and to her disappointment, they were already open.

Am I…in bed? Really?

Apparently she was. The noxious pink bed-curtains were drawn around her, although the light coming through them was darker and bloodier than she had ever seen. She sat up and pulled one aside.

"I knew you'd come back to me," said the green-eyed man, sitting down on the edge of the bed. "I knew you wouldn't leave without helping me."

The shadows cast across his skin were dark, almost purple. When Bryony peered past him to the window, she saw a tangle of leaves and thorns.

"I'm dreaming," she said. "The windows. I saw that in my dreams. You're from my dreams, too."

He smiled. "You are not exactly dreaming. There are great magics breaking loose, and they let me come to you here, close to the waking world."

He reached out and stroked her shoulder. Bryony realized that she was wearing a thin nightgown and not much else.

Did the wind change my clothes? Where is Holly? Did any of yesterday happen at all, or is this a very long strange dream?

The green-eyed man knelt on the bed beside her, his hands moving slowly down her body. Bryony shuddered convulsively. It felt as if he had touched her in some deep, impossible place, touched her and stroked her intimately. Her body throbbed in response, and the green-eyed man smiled.

Wait—wait—

She had been wanting this for weeks. And yet this had happened before, hadn't it? He'd touch her and leave her aching, and then there would be only waking and emptiness—

Those were dreams. You know, the same dreams where he yelled at you for talking to the Beast.

She pulled away from him. She needed a minute, just a minute, just one, where he wasn't touching her with that scalding touch.

"Poor thing," he murmured. "Afraid? After all the dreams? Even now?"

She didn't much like being called "poor thing." She hadn't liked it before, either.

She stared up into his eyes.

They were green, as green as leaves, and now that he was so close, she saw something that she'd never noticed before.

The pupils of his eyes were not black. They were dark burgundy, the color of rose-leaves emerging in spring.

Something clicked inside her head.

She hadn't told Holly the right things. Holly wasn't a gardener, and she didn't have enough information to guess.

"You're the rose," said Bryony. "I don't know how, but *you're* the wild rose."

He laughed out loud, and Bryony pulled back a little farther. There was something not quite right about that laugh.

"Figured it out at last, have you?" he said, reaching out and trailing a finger down her arm. The touch stung like a thorn and made Bryony gasp.

Stop that. Stop that. Dear God, how is this happening? I love plants, but not like that!

It's magic. It's some kind of magic. He's been getting into my dreams and doing this—and I thought it was just a dream, and I let him!

"You're—*how* are you the rose?" She sat up, pulling the sheets up to her chest. His eyes gleamed.

"Everything has a spirit, poor little Bryony. Even things that humans don't notice. Some of us are stronger than others. Some of us do very foolish things, and sell their—I suppose you would say their *soul*—to others of us." He grinned. It was the first time that Bryony had seen him grin.

His teeth were very white, but the canines had the flat, hooked shape of rose thorns.

"What have you done to the Beast?"

The rose's eyes narrowed. "He's outlived his time. You should stay here with me. We could do so much together, you and I…"

He grabbed her hair. His nails had pale green cuticles.

There were a lot of clues. I just didn't notice them because hey, it was a dream! Holly was right, I am an idiot.

"Stop touching me," she growled, even though her skin was burning and she was shaking so hard she thought she might fly apart. "Go away. *Stop.*"

"Still longing for your Beast?" crooned the rose. "I could look like him, you know. If that's what you really wanted."

His shape began to change, to grow into a dark shape with fur the color of a newly unfurled rose leaf. Her room had always smelled of roses but now it was thick and cloying and that was wrong, the Beast should smell like cloves and fur, this wasn't the Beast, this wasn't even a dream, this was *horrible*—

Her knife was gone from her thigh. The only thing left to her was simple human strength, and God knew what use it would be against a monster.

It's trying to get out, the Beast had said, and she had been too stupid and too slow to figure out what he was talking about.

He was right. She *should* have come back with fire and an army.

Still, she was here at last, even if it was too little, even if it was far too late.

"You're not the Beast!" she cried to the rose. "I don't want anything to do with you! Go away!"

She punched him in the face.

She had been slinging mulch for nearly three years now, and digging holes, and moving compost. Bryony the gardener was much stronger than Bryony the merchant's daughter would have been.

Even that might not have been much use against the wild rose creature, but she hit him with the hand that had the silver ring on it.

He fell back from the ring, screaming. It left a dark mark across the half-formed face that spread out. She smelled burning leaves. He staggered backwards, off the bed.

"You shouldn't have done that." His voice was muffled. There was blood oozing between his fingers, but it was the wrong color.

I didn't hit him that hard, I couldn't hit someone that hard, it's the ring, the ring did something, what did it do, is it because it's silver or the Beast's or—

At the window he stopped. She heard glass break, and rose canes came through, wrapping around him like a lover. He lifted his ruined face—half human, half Beast, framed in roses, and stared at her with savage green eyes.

"Stupid thing," he hissed, and was gone.

Bryony stayed in the bed for longer than was probably safe. The rose leaves chattered together at the window, and the room was lit with that dark, bloody light.

Staying in bed is stupid. Bed isn't safe. You're just in the habit of thinking that monsters can't get you as long as you're in the bed.

No knife. No shoes. Wearing a nightgown. Fighting a wild rose— what? Spirit? Monster? God only knows. No help for it. Have to find the Beast.

I hope Holly's okay.

"House," she said out loud, "I've never been quite sure what you are. Some of you is pretty clearly bad. But some of you I've always liked, and I hope you're still there." She closed her eyes. "If you're there, if there's anything left of you that's good, I need your help."

She gripped the sheets. She had a sense that something was listening. It wasn't the awful listening silence, but some small, wounded animal presence.

"I need my clothes," she said. "I will do my very best to help you and the Beast. I need my clothes, and my gloves, and my pruning shears."

An enchanted rose spirit might not be a gardening problem exactly, but she was a gardener and that was the only set of solutions she knew.

A little breeze sighed. The sheets seemed to settle a little differently.

She opened her eyes and there were her clothes by the foot of the bed. Her gloves lay across them, crossing the gleaming arc of her pruning shears.

No boots.

Well, you couldn't have everything.

The blankets tried to straighten themselves and fell back, exhausted. Whatever part of House was trying to help her, it seemed to be on its last legs.

She dressed hurriedly under the sheets, not wanting the roses at the window to see her naked. *And wow, that would have been* quite *insane yesterday, wouldn't it?*

The shears she slid into the loop at her waist. She pulled on the gloves.

It's a rose. A big rose. You'll never chop it all down with hand tools. You could burn it out, maybe, but you'll take House out with it.

Would that be such a bad thing?

She'd hate to kill the good with the bad, but if that was what was required to reach the Beast…

Getting out of bed was hard. The darkness under the bed seemed huge. She had gone seventeen years knowing that there was a monster there, waiting to grab her, and if that was true of the gentle, dusty shadows under her own bad at home, what horrors would be lurking under *this* bed, in this bloody, rust-colored light?

"I don't have time for this," she growled. "The Beast needs me." She swung her feet out and put them on the floor.

She made one step towards the door when something reached out from under the bed and grabbed her.

CHAPTER THIRTY

All the times that Bryony had imagined something reaching out from under the bed and latching onto her ankles, she had never actually imagined what happened next.

If she had given it any thought at all, it would be to assume that she would die neatly and immediately of heart failure, and that would be the end of it.

But she did not die. Her heart gave a panicky squeeze and she fell flat on her face, but she did not die. Her pulse galloped and her ankles exploded with pain as something stabbed into them—but she still did not die.

She grabbed for the carpet and the edge of the nightstand and looked over her shoulder.

Oh God, oh God, it'll be hands with claws, big long claws, big huge scaly hands—

It was rose stems.

Two long whips had wrapped around her ankles, like a climbing rose clawing its way up a fence. Thorns sank deeply into her skin. They dragged at her, pulling her backward—not under the bed, but toward the window, she thought.

Terrified, furious, and in a great deal of pain, she nevertheless began to laugh.

"Oh no," she said. "Oh no, you don't get to do that. Not to *me.*"

She let go of the carpet and grabbed the shears off her belt. They fit into her hand the way that her knife never had.

Much more useful for this sort of thing anyway.

She reached down and cut through the first stem.

The rose *keened*—there was no other word for it—and the cut end whipped around like a snake. It made a high hurting sound and the leaves in the window rustled and thrashed.

Wherever the green-eyed man was, she hoped that had hurt him, too.

She sawed through the other stem. This one was tougher and stringier and twisted under the blade. Blood trickled down over her feet.

When I finally get out of here, if I make it to the staircase, I'm gonna slip on my own blood and crack my skull open on the marble. Hopefully Holly will get to the Beast in time.

She pried the thorny ends out of her skin and staggered to her feet. Once cut, the roses lay dead and innocent in her hands.

She stalked to the door.

It didn't want to open at first. She hammered on it with the handles of the shears and snapped "House! Open the damn door!"

Whether the part of the house that was still her friend responded, or whether it was the threat of the shears (and what was she going to do to an entire *house* with them, anyway? Cut it off at the root cellar?) the door creaked open.

She stepped out into a hallway. It wasn't the one that it should be. There were windows lining this one, and no staircase or landing in sight. Through the windows streamed that bloody fractured light, lying in red bars across the floor.

Bryony exhaled.

"Beast?" she called. "Beast, where *are* you? Are you in here?"

There was no reply. Wherever the Beast was, either he couldn't hear her, or couldn't come.

She had a sick feeling in the pit of her stomach that it was the latter. What had he said, so long ago?

If you have need of me at any time, you have only to call my name. If it is within my power to come to you, I will.

She had called him. He had not come. Therefore, wherever the Beast was in this wretched place, it was not within his power to come to her.

Therefore, I will go to him.

The hallway beckoned. She walked toward the first window. It was covered in branches and roses, with the red light shining through them.

I could break it out and climb out. I could probably hack back some of the roses. Would that help? Is he going to be outside?

Bryony eyed the thicket of roses grimly. *I'm on the second floor, or something like it. Perhaps I should go back to my own window and chop through that. Then I could get into the courtyard, at least.*

When she turned, her door was no longer behind her. The corridor went in both directions.

"Playing tricks on me, rose?" she asked grimly. "Very well." She strode forward, her feet burning and stabbing with each step.

At the second window, she glanced to the side, but this one was bound even more thickly. So was the third.

She hurried on, flicking her gaze sideways to the windows, hurrying as fast as her bloodied feet would carry her. If the light faded (and surely it was sunset by now) then she would be running through a dark hallway.

At the fifth or sixth or seventh window, something changed.

Bryony snapped her head around so quickly that a muscle in her neck twinged, because there was someone in the window.

It was a human.

Had been a human.

She had no idea how long it had been there. The skin looked parched and mummified. It wore the rags of servant's livery, but they had been torn apart by a thicket of rose canes bursting out of its chest. Its mouth hung open, and more rose stems grew from it, forcing it into a silent scream.

There was almost nothing in her stomach, but she staggered two steps and threw up until she was empty of even the memory of food.

That's it. That's it. I don't know if it's real or not, I don't know what's going on, but if I get home and get out of this, I'm going to rip every goddamn rose bush in the garden out by the roots and burn *them.*

She crawled forward on her hands and knees, trying not to look up, but of course at the next window she did look up, and there were two bodies, bound together by the wicked embrace of the roses.

She closed her eyes after that and crawled along the floor like a blind beetle, leaving smears of blood behind her.

How the rose would laugh if he could see her now.

Probably he could see her. Undoubtedly he was laughing. The sounds of the rose tapping at the windows was very much like laughter.

"Oh Beast," she moaned. "Oh Beast, I want to find you. Help me. Get me out of this place. *Please.*"

She got up eventually, keeping her eyes on the floor. When she looked up, which she did occasionally, even knowing what she would see, the wild rose spirit had arranged tableaus in the window, most of them obscene. Dead lovers penetrated one another with rose whips, were torn apart and chained together by them, in extraordinary variation.

"The rose," she said, dropping her eyes to the carpet, "is a *bastard.*"

This was such an incredible understatement and she was so numbed by horrors that she began to laugh again. It was hacking, sobbing laughter, but it was definitely laughter all the same.

The roses clawed at the windows. She could see the shadows writhing on the floor. Apparently her laughter infuriated the rose, and that only made her laugh harder, and gave her the strength to climb to her feet.

"I won't look at you," she told the windows. "If those were ever real people, you're a murderer, and if not, you're very sick, and if I can lay my hands on about eight hundred gallons of vinegar, I will sear your roots until you wither away to nothing. But I still won't look."

She walked on, and did not look.

The roses smashed against the glass in fury, but the glass held. Perhaps there was some strength left to House after all.

She had no idea how long she walked down that hall. No more than a few minutes, most likely. It felt like a hundred years.

Horrible things always seem like they're taking longer. Unless this really is taking longer and my sense of time is confused as well...

If the Beast was indeed functionally immortal, perhaps that wouldn't matter.

Funny, it had never occurred to her to ask if she was functionally immortal while staying in the house either. Holly would have pounced on that immediately.

She hoped that Holly was safe. Had the rose seen her? Had she made it to the Beast's manor at all?

A new noise intruded into her awareness, a soft ticking sound, like a very small clock.

She looked up, and then to one side—not the side with the windows—and then finally it occurred to her to look down.

The clockwork bee was trundling down the hall toward her.

A little bubble of relief rose in her throat. She let out a single hacking sob and clenched her fists against her breast to keep from making another.

The bee crept toward her, *tick-tick-tick.*

Bryony knelt down, watching the little brass legs move, one after another, until it finally bumped into her knee.

"Did the Beast send you?" she asked.

The bee backed up a step, its antennae moving. It whirred its wings and rose an inch or two off the ground, then tumbled back to the carpet, unmoving.

Holly picked it up and wound the infinitesimal key, listening to the small, friendly sound it made, *zzzip, zzzip, zzzip,* the only sound in that long hallway except for her breathing.

She released the key and held her breath.

It whirred its wings and took off. It circled her head once, twice, as if she were a puzzling flower, then landed on the carpet again.

Then it turned around and began walking away from her.

Bryony followed.

Walking is easier than flying, she thought, as the bee trundled determinedly forward, a little gleam of light in the darkened hall. She followed. The bee was very slow compared to a walking human, but not so bad compared to a limping one.

She had followed it perhaps five minutes, ignoring forty or fifty windows, and the clockwork bee stopped. Its antennae spun. It turned ninety degrees and walked toward a door.

The door did not open. Bryony slammed the heel of her hand on it, and then the shears. The doorframe shivered.

"House," she said. *"House!"*

The bee walked into the door, spun its antennae, backed up and tried again. Finding no entrance, it began to climb up the doorframe.

"House!" cried Bryony, beating on the frame with the shears.

The wood groaned, as if two forces struggled inside it, one trying to force it open and one determined to hold it shut. Bryony threw her shoulder against it, and it moved, grudgingly.

It got half an inch open, then stopped, but that was enough. She jammed the shears into the gap and hauled on them, using the wooden handles as a lever *and if they break, I am in a world of hurt.*

But they did not break. The door opened onto a flight of stairs.

She had never seen these stairs before. They were narrow and steep, the sort of back stairs used by servants, or by merchant's daughters escaping from their nurses. She scooped up the bee and put it in a pocket (its legs kicked wildly) and flung herself down them at breakneck speed.

The door at the bottom was gone, but the doorway was filled with roses.

They lay like a nest of serpents across the floor. Flowers bloomed extravagantly beside thorns as long as Bryony's fingers. A sweet scent filled the stairwell until she thought that she might choke on it.

She still had her gloves. She pulled her shirt up over her nose and mouth to drown out the stink of roses. The smell of sweaty terrified human cut through it nicely. She grabbed the first stem and began to cut.

Pruning roses, even ordinary, decent roses, is slow work. Even the kindest of rosebushes does not yield easily to the knife.

These were worse. Worse than briars, worse than brambles, worse than thickets of wild blackberry.

Her leather gloves were cut and punctured by thorns. Blood ran down her arms from scratches, and sap matted down her hair. She hacked at stems as thick as her wrist, sawing at them with the edge of the shears, sometimes crying with frustration, sometimes laughing with relief.

If I get through this, these shears are done.

If I get through this, I will have them repaired and hung over the fireplace, like an old campaigner's sword.

It was surely her imagination that towards the end, the stems became easier to cut, as if the rose were retreating. But she sawed through the last stem, a monstrous tangle that wrapped around itself two or three times, and when she looked up, the doorway was clear.

She stepped out into the courtyard at the heart of the manor.

CHAPTER THIRTY-ONE

The first thing she saw was the Beast.

He was standing beside the birch tree. Bryony ran forward, heedless of the rose stems that coiled across the flagstones. "Beast! Beast, you're—"

Her throat closed.

He was not standing after all. He was hanging suspended in a tangle of roses. The bushes that had surrounded the tree had grown upwards, coiling around the white trunk and scrambling into the lowest limbs. The birch's leaves were thin and skeletal. The Beast hung silently below them, with rose canes wrapped around his arms and wrists and across his chest. His robe hung in tatters.

And after all my work pruning those damn bushes, she thought, absurdly irritated, because the alternative would be to look too closely at the Beast and actually comprehend the horror of the situation.

The rose bushes had buckled and cracked the flagstones around the base of the birch tree. There was no clear path through them, but Bryony had not particularly expected one.

"Listen to me, wild rose," she growled, lifting her abused shears. "You can let me through, or I can hack my way through. It's up to you."

The rose leaves clattered with mocking laughter. Bryony shook her head. "All right, if that's the way it is…"

She started cutting. The rose keened in pain and retreated before her. Stems writhed away.

"I warned you," she panted. There was room enough now to get one foot on the flagstones at the base of the birch. She jammed her foot in. A rose thorn struck at it, and she sliced the whole whip off at the base, cursing.

She was on the third stem—or the thirtieth—when something came chattering out of the dark at her.

She saw it out of the corner of her eye, a big dark shape, moving fast, and jerked back, raising the shears to hold it off.

There was nothing there.

I'm hallucinating. I'm seeing things that aren't there.

There are so many things that are actually here, it seems like a waste to start inventing more…

She went back to chopping. She had barely set the shears to another stem when another thing came at her, something with a suggestion of teeth and eyes and fury, and she had to whip around and face empty air.

Her neck gave a bright spasm of pain. The rose leaves snickered.

"You're doing this," said Bryony aloud. She gritted her teeth and went back to sawing.

Unfortunately, knowing that the rose was doing it didn't help as much as it could have. Bryony knew that the shapes weren't real, but her spine and her nerves and the back of her brain didn't believe it. When the shadows jumped, so did she.

Her progress cutting through the rose slowed to a crawl.

This is stupid. They're not real. It can't stop me with real briars, so it's stopping me with fake monsters. This is stupid.

Claws rose in the air and a shadow leaped at her and Bryony gritted her teeth, trying not to jump and closed her eyes…

"This is not beautiful," said a voice that wasn't really there either. "This is inelegant. A fair maiden saving her beloved, that is fine, that is the very essence of poetry, but this is *not* acceptable."

"Irving?" whispered Bryony.

In her mind's eye, the poet looked down his nose at her. "None other. I do *not* approve of the garden shears, by the way."

"You wouldn't," said Bryony, smiling, and thought, *I've lost my mind, but that's okay, my mind wasn't helping much anyway.*

She opened her eyes and tackled another stem. A shape leapt for her, and another shape stepped in to stop it.

"Halt!" cried the poet. "You shall not interfere in love's great work! Back, curs! The pen is mightier than the sword, but the sword has its uses still!"

Bryony still could barely make out details, but the shape in the corner of her eye did look as if it were wearing a puffy white shirt, and it did seem to be waving a sword.

This is magic. Or madness. Perhaps there's no real difference.

The rose screamed in rage. She didn't know if it was inside or outside her head. The shapes were fewer and slower and Irving drove them away before they could break her concentration.

"I shall give you such a beating, fiends, as you will bear back with you to the Pit! Tell them that Matthias Irving sent you!"

The Beast had not moved all this time. She wasn't even sure he was breathing. If she got to him and found that she was cutting down a corpse—well, best not to think of that.

She cleared enough space for her other foot. The shears were so dull and streaked with sap that she was forced to saw at the thicker stems.

Much more of this and I'll be using my teeth...

The birch tree was leaning sideways and one of its roots had heaved up out of the dirt. Bryony stepped up onto it.

Birch tree and wild rose. If we live through this, I'll have to get the Beast to explain to me how they fit together.

She reached out and caught the Beast's wrist and nearly wept with relief, because he was warm. There was a pulse, too fast, too weak, but a pulse nonetheless, and hers probably wouldn't be doing much better if she were hanging from a possessed rose bush.

"Come on, Beast," she said, standing on tiptoes and grabbing one of his ears. "Come *on*. Don't do anything stupid. I've got this far, but I need your help!"

A shudder went through him and he lifted his head from his chest. His nostrils flared, and then his golden eyes slowly cracked open.

"Bryony...?"

She laughed out loud.

"What...what're you...not supposed to be here..."

"Yes, well." Bryony kissed his cheek. The fur on his face was fine and flat and did not feel all that different from kissing a human, and she wondered why she'd waited so long to do it.

"What...?"

"Next time," she said, crouching down and sawing at the rose stems wrapped around his legs, "next time *warn* me if going away means that the roses get to eat you. What a colossal mess."

He thrashed weakly. "You...no. Get *away*. The rose...you have to get away from the rose." His breath ran out on a long sigh. "Should never have tried to keep you here. Didn't know...it had gotten...so *strong.*"

"It's a problem with wild rose thickets," agreed Bryony. "They form these stands if you don't pull them out soon enough, and then it's a serious job." She stood up again and went to work on his left arm. "Hold still, or I'll take chunks out of you on accident. This isn't a precision instrument."

"Not just a rose..." The Beast pulled his arm free and began tearing at the thorns. Bryony smacked him on the forearm.

"Stop that! I'll get you out."

"Have to hurry," said the Beast. "It's not just the rose. It's more than a rose. It's a spirit. It's completely mad—"

"We've met," said Bryony shortly. "Couple of times now."

The rose leaves clattered and hissed around her, whispering obscenities.

A rim of white showed around the Beast's eyes.

"If he couldn't take me by myself, he can't possibly take the two of us," said Bryony, with a lot more authority than she felt. "The house is helping."

The Beast shook his head. "The house is dying," he rasped. "She's the birch tree. You understand?"

"Not even a little," said Bryony. She sliced through the last stem and threw the severed length aside.

The Beast took a shuffling step sideways and swept her up in his arms. Bryony squeaked in surprise.

"You came back," he said hoarsely. His face was buried in her shoulder. He had quite a lot of face, so this covered a lot of territory and meant that a tusk was poking her in the collarbone, but Bryony didn't particularly mind.

"Of course I did," she said. "You're my Beast, and I love you."

The roses screamed.

It was a good thing that the Beast was so tall, because otherwise Bryony was fairly sure they would have perished right then. The whole thicket thrashed and writhed around them, striking out with thorny whips, and only the Beast's fur and the fact that he literally held Bryony up over his head saved them from being flayed alive.

He swung her over top of the rampaging thorns and stepped over the thicket himself. Bryony clung to his arms, feeling like a very small creature indeed.

A crack like thunder sounded above them, and she looked up in time to see several bricks separate from the manor house and come crashing to the ground.

"That seems bad," said Bryony.

"I apologize for this," said the Beast, and slung her around his back. She just had time to grab onto the collar of his robe, and he dropped to all fours and charged through the whipping sea of thorns.

The doorways out of the courtyard were not open, but it rapidly didn't matter, because the house was falling apart anyway. Part of the wall fell down in front of them.

Oh, House…

The Beast slammed through the hole into a hallway, twisted to avoid a toppling door, and went out the other side. Bryony had a suspicion that even in its death-throes, the house was trying to help them. They skidded down a long, shuddering hall, masonry crashing down behind them, but the Beast stayed ahead of the beams, and a door fell down in front of them and opened the way to the outside again.

The roses were waiting for them, striking like snakes, but the Beast leapt and twisted and Bryony clung tight, not letting go even when a whip cracked across her head and tore a hank of hair (and a bit of scalp) out with it.

"The garden!" she yelled at him. "Find the garden!"

She didn't know why she said that—maybe nothing more than the hope that her shovel would still be there, or another set of shears—but the Beast took it as an order. He cleared the remnants of the boxwood hedge with one bound and tore towards the far corner of the lawn.

Her first thought was that the rose had gotten here first, and she felt a sick wrench of betrayal. Sure, the wild rose was a plant, but these were hers! She'd taken care of them! They came from her very own garden! So why was there a stand of leaves, as tall as a small tree, where her little garden had been?

Then the Beast reached the edge of the leaves, and she understood.

Her garden had grown. The roses were shoving at the edges, trying to jam thorns through, and her plants were fighting back.

Sage grew six feet in the air, reinforced by a wall of lamb's-ear at her feet and tied together with the climbing stems of peas. Leaves of basil six inches long formed glossy pillars, threaded with the narrow lances of verbena. Where thorns tore at them, the smell was thick and herbal and cut through the cloying sweetness of the rose.

And underground, forming an impenetrable wall against the suckers of even the most determined wild rose...

The rutabagas were the size of her head. Their white and purple crowns gleamed against the dark earth.

"Oh, my dears…" she said, her voice cracking. "Did any gardener ever have such friends?" She slid off the Beast's back and ran forward. The roses nearest to her tried to strike, but were muffled under a coat of oregano as thick as the Beast's fur.

"Looks like everything but the radishes," she said, laughing and wiping at her eyes. "And you can't expect much combat out of radishes."

She laid a hand on the thickly knotted stems of sage and they opened with a soft rustle of leaves.

She stepped through. The Beast followed her. The opening in the leaves knit together behind him.

Through the gap, just before it closed, she saw a figure in a white shirt lift its sword in salute.

Irving. Thank you. For everything.

CHAPTER THIRTY-TWO

"Do you think we'll be safe here?" she asked, turning to the Beast.

"From the rose, possibly," said the Beast. "From your sister, I'm not so sure."

He bowed very deeply, and Holly, who had come around the side of the herb wheel with her butcher knife raised, stopped and pretended that she hadn't been about to stab anyone.

"You must be Holly," he said.

"And you must be the Beast," she said.

"She's a very good guesser," said Bryony, putting a hand on the Beast's arm.

"So I see."

"Three of us in one family may be entirely too much for comfort," said Holly. She scowled at the Beast. "I'm still angry at you, but we'll get to that later. Bryony, what the hell happened? One minute I had hold of you, and the next I feel like I've been turned inside out and I land in the middle of this." She waved the knife at the garden. "I stuck my head out, but there were some really *angry* plants out there, so I thought I'd stay here and see if you turned up or if I needed to stage a rescue."

"It is the rose spirit," said the Beast, sitting down on the grass. "It is very angry."

"You're going to have to explain *everything,*" said Bryony.

He sighed. "What I can, I will. A long time ago, when I was young and human, I went hunting. A boar killed my horse, and I was wounded, and went staggering through the woods like a fool, until I wandered into a grove of sacred trees."

Possibly because she was a gardener, Bryony had no trouble imagining sacred trees. Holly raised an eyebrow, but that was all.

"The spirit there took pity on me," said the Beast. "Pity of a sort, anyway. She took human form and nursed me until I was well again. But she fell in love with me, and I—well, I was a fool. I did not think that I could love a birch tree, so I spurned her."

"A full-on spurning?" said Holly. "Goodness. No wonder she was upset." Bryony elbowed her in the ribs.

The Beast rubbed his arms, as if chilled under his fur. "In the wilds, there are many spirits, and some of them are very powerful. She went to a wild rose spirit, an old and dangerous one, and offered him all of her power to punish me. To possess me. I don't think she was quite sure which herself. The rose accepted."

Outside the protective ring of plants, there was a loud crash, as if a wing of the manor had collapsed entirely.

"As for me, I went to bed inside my hunting lodge, and woke up in the manor house. I believe it was a place that had existed before, that the rose found abandoned, but I am not sure. My servants were gone." He sighed. "I wish that I could believe they escaped, but there were things—the house would cook some dishes like my cook had, and those dresses you wore—I cannot believe that there was nothing human behind them. I believe the rose and the tree absorbed them in some fashion. It is why the house could read a little, and why it understood some things and not others…" He ran a clawed hand over his face, and Bryony thought of the shapes in servant's livery that she had seen through the windows, violated by the rose.

A moment passed, and then the Beast picked up the thread again. "I was as you see me. The birch spirit came to me and said that as I did not believe I could love one who was not human, so I would be unhuman myself, until I found love in return." He laughed softly. "I believe that she intended to force me into accepting her affections but—well—"

"Well?" asked Holly.

He shrugged. "I went a little mad, honestly. By the time it subsided, the poor birch had come to realize what had happened. She and I were trapped here, and the rose with us. The rose fed on her strength and forced her spirit into the walls of the house, where she could not fight back. And I fear that houses are very different than humans, and so by the time I had learned to talk and walk upright again, the birch had fallen quite decisively out of love with me."

Holly snorted. Bryony put a hand over her eyes. "Poor Beast!"

"It would have been a dreadful blow to my ego, but...well." He sighed. "The truth is, I forgave her long ago, and she me. We are both of us prisoners. I was young and arrogant, and she was young and hurt, and we have both paid the price a thousand times over."

"And the girl who killed herself..." said Bryony.

"Her name was Beauty." He sighed. "I was still arrogant. I thought that if I could have someone here, in time they would understand what had happened. In time they might love me. I learned my mistake very quickly, but I did not correct it in time."

"I wonder if she dreamed about a green-eyed man," said Bryony.

The Beast looked up. "A what?"

"The rose. I dreamed about a man with green eyes. He kept asking me to help him. He was very...persuasive."

He looked at her intently, with those endless gold eyes. Bryony sighed.

"I thought maybe he was you," she said. "That you were under some enchantment and you were trying to talk to me in dreams. By the time I'd realized that it wasn't you..."

She slumped down next to him on the grass.

"Ah," he said. "No." He reached out and covered her hand with his own. "Do not blame yourself. I did not realize until too late that the footsteps in your room were the rose, and that it was doing it deliberately to frighten you. I should have realized it long before, but it was a spirit, and I did not think that it would take the shape of a man. I should have guessed."

"Well," said Holly, "not to interrupt all the recriminations, but *now* what?"

"Can you leave now, Beast?" asked Bryony. "I don't know how long the garden will hold. If we can get over the wall, maybe we can come back with a whole lot of fire and vinegar." She considered. "And salt. And hedge clippers. And maybe a couple of teams of oxen to hook to the roots of the rose and tear it out. And probably priests."

"Huh!" Holly shoved her butcher knife into her belt. "Good luck with our priest. You'd be better off with nuns. The convent might be able to do something."

"I'm not sure if I can leave," said the Beast. "Unless—Bryony—"

He turned to her, and took both her hands. His eyes were beautiful and golden and his face was hideous and Bryony loved him.

"Bryony, I know what you said before, and I realize, it may not be enough—or you might not mean it quite like that, but—will you marry me?"

"You didn't do that *already?*" cried Holly, throwing her hands in the air. "Dear God!"

"Holly," said Bryony severely, "I have had a *very* long day, possibly the longest day of my entire life and I have been cut to ribbons on magic roses and saw some really unpleasant things in the windows and been attacked by shadows and ruined a really excellent pair of shears and this is furthermore the only marriage proposal I am likely to get because I intend to accept it, so why don't you go away for a few minutes so that I can enjoy it?"

Holly gave the Beast a look. "Are you sure you want to deal with this?"

"Of course I—" Bryony began.

"Wasn't talking to *you.*"

The Beast grinned. "I have found that it is best, at such times, to simply accept the inevitable."

"You'll do," said Holly. "Fine! I'm going! I'll be over here, waiting for the roses to come kill us all."

She stalked over to the other side of the herb wheel. Since the plants on it had not grown explosively the way that the others had, even the tallest was only about knee-high.

"And you can look the other way, too," said Bryony.

"Yes, yes…"

Bryony turned back to the Beast. He smiled down at her.

"Beast, I would love to marry you."

Something exploded.

At first Bryony thought it was somewhere in the garden, and then she thought perhaps it was inside her head. The world went grey and distant, the way that it had when she was travelling between the manor house and her own cottage. Bryony could feel the Beast's hands holding hers, and she clung to them. The silver ring on her finger blazed with heat, but it was a kind heat, and warmed the space between them.

Somewhere she could hear the rose screaming.

Silvery light broke up the greyness. It did not so much illuminate as sharpen, so that when Bryony looked for the source, she saw it clearly, while the world around it was pushed back into shadows.

It was the silver-haired woman.

"You!" said Bryony. "I dreamed about you!"

The woman smiled ruefully. "Yes," she said. "Although I should not have come to your dreams, for it forged a channel that the rose could use as well. But perhaps all will yet end for the best."

The Beast rose to his feet, still holding Bryony's hand, and bowed to the woman in silver. "It has been a long time," he said. "It is good to see you again, even under these conditions."

The woman smiled. Her eyes were the color of birch leaves, and Bryony could have kicked herself for not realizing the truth sooner. "You were the good bits of House, weren't you?" she asked. "Thank you. You were very kind."

The birch tree smiled, a little ruefully. "It was not all me. Without the minds of the servants that we took so long ago, I would have been a very poor host. Ah, those poor souls. They were innocent, and we did badly by them." She shook herself, and Bryony seemed to hear the rattle of birch leaves. "But all is not yet done, and we must hurry, for I am dying."

The Beast made a sound of pain.

The birch tree lifted a pale hand. "No, no. I am ready for it. Trees are good at dying, you know, we practice it for many autumns. It is time, and more than time."

A rustle ran through the garden, hundreds of leaves moving softly in acknowledgement. Bryony moved closer to the Beast.

"There is power when a tree-spirit dies," said the birch tree. "Even an old and broken one like me. And the rose is vulnerable at this moment, with the severing of its enchantments. I shall die, and take the rose with me. It will destroy the house, but it will be gone. Though I do not suggest that you try to live here any more, either of you."

"I would prefer never to see this place again," said Bryony.

Beast exhaled slowly. "I do not know if I should leave it," he said. "Will I regain my human form?"

"You have been here for nearly two hundred years," said the birch gently. "I could give you your human shape back, yes. And all those years would come due at once, and you would be dead before you passed the gates."

"No!" said Bryony, gripping the Beast's shoulder. *Like the brother and sister turned into a swan,* she thought. *I could not stand it if he turned to dust in front of me. It is not fair that I won him back from the rose to lose him ten minutes later.*

"It need not be," the birch assured her. "You will no longer be immortal, Beast, but you will wear your age lightly. There is at least a normal human span left to you, if not a little more."

"That's fine," said Bryony. "With me, anyway. Beast?"

"I have lived longer than I wished," said the Beast, "but I find that I am not quite eager to die yet. But are you sure?" He glanced down at Bryony. "It will not be easy, I imagine, living with a monster."

"If you don't mind being a Beast then I certainly don't mind being with one. Truth be told, if you turned into a human, I'd have a hard time getting used to it." She grinned. "And if any of the townspeople complain, we'll set Holly on them."

"Then I have no fears at all for the future," said the Beast, and turned to the birch tree. He nodded.

The silver-haired woman smiled. "Let it be so," she said, in her old, creaking voice. "And if the blessing of a tree matters, may you have many, many springs together."

She turned away from them, and lifted a hand. The plants in Bryony's garden parted before her, bowing down as if before their queen.

Through the gap in the wall of leaves, Bryony saw the green-eyed man. He was no longer beautiful. His skin had gone grey and weathered, and his hair had turned to dry, brittle stalks. He lifted his head and snarled at the birch woman.

She walked toward him and put her arms around him. He shuddered, and seemed to sink into himself.

"Come," said the birch tree to the wild rose, "it's time to go."

CHAPTER THIRTY-THREE

When Bryony regained consciousness, she was lying on the Beast's chest in the middle of the garden.

It was warm and rather pleasant, but even the most comfortably padded lover has ribs and elbows and so forth, so she sat up reluctantly. The Beast smiled up at her and climbed to his feet.

"About time you two got up," said Holly, poking her head around the corner of the hedge. "I didn't get much of a look at it before, but this place has really gone to hell in a handbasket."

Bryony and the Beast, hand in hand, went to look.

The manor house had fallen in on itself. Great holes had been torn in the masonry, and fallen beams lay strewn like bones. The roses that had climbed across the front porch were not just skeletal but charred and black.

"Well," said Bryony. "I don't think we'll be living here any time soon."

The Beast frowned. "I would just as soon never see this place again. If we can reach my workshop, there are a few things that I would like to retrieve, but otherwise it may fall into ruins with my blessing."

It took them most of the morning to locate the workshop. The Beast had lost none of his strength with the ending of the enchantment, and he pulled stones loose bare-handed that would have taken Bryony a crowbar and a hard day's labor.

The workshop was partly intact. The back had fallen down and one wall leaned crazily inward, but there were tools scattered around the floor, still gleaming brightly. The Beast swept as many as he could find into a makeshift sack made of his old robe, and slung it over his shoulder.

He surveyed the ruins and sighed. "I would like to have buried the servants," he said. "If there is anything left of them after all this time. But I don't know where they might be, or how to start looking. I hope that they passed quickly and without pain."

Bryony remembered the bodies in the windows and kept her mouth shut.

"I'm surprised so much survived," said Holly. "The rest of this place looks as if it's been abandoned for centuries."

"The original house had been," said the Beast, "and now it is reverting, I expect. But I made most of these tools myself, with my own labor instead of magic, and so they have survived."

"If you can carry a *bit* more," said Bryony, "if you don't mind terribly—"

"I will carry you to the ends of the earth if that's what you wish, love."

Bryony ignored Holly's rolled eyes. "I can't bring all the plants home, I know, and I hope that some of them will sink their roots here and make it their home. But I can't just *leave* them. Not after they worked so hard to save me."

"Completely understandable," said the Beast, and stood patiently while Bryony loaded him down like a pack mule with a dozen transplants: the sage and the lamb's-ears and the opportunistic oregano.

In one last way, the birch had helped her. Those plants that had moved aside under her hand had gone to seed as if it were high summer.

Well, she had been a tree. Trees understood these things, presumably, as well or better than gardeners.

So Bryony harvested the seeds of the faithful rutabagas, the basil and verbena, and tucked them away, first into the little pouches that Iris had made for her, so long ago, and then, when those were full, into scraps of paper torn from the books that House had made and printed with gibberish.

She left the rest of the annuals to their fate. "I hope you re-seed," she told them. "I hope you re-seed a *lot,* and if anybody ever finds this place, it'll be wall-to-wall basil and peas and there won't be a scrap of lawn left. I hope they find *weeds.*"

And then she scrubbed her cheeks with both hands and turned away, trying not to feel as if she were abandoning her friends.

"This is how it starts, you know," Holly told the Beast. "She'll have you out turning compost heaps and digging up rocks before you know it."

"I hope so," said the Beast. "I eat a great deal, after all."

Bryony leaned her cheek against his arm. "I will grow lots of vegetables," she promised. "And we will build you a workshop so that you can make little clockwork creatures."

"I wish I was as certain as you are that your villagers will welcome a Beast," said the Beast.

"They will deal with it," said Holly. "And if they do not deal with it, *I* will deal with *them.*"

"It will work out," said Bryony firmly. She reached out and took his hand. It was very large and rather furry, but the fingers that curled around hers were warm and alive. She squeezed and he squeezed back.

She and the Beast walked hand in hand through the ruined gates, and into the world beyond them.

ACKNOWLEDGMENTS

Every time I write one of these acknowledgment thingies, I am amazed that books ever get written at all.

I wrote this one as I write most of mine—I started somewhere, fiddled with it off and on for a year or two, and then suddenly finished it off in a mad sprint to the end. For whatever odd reason, that mad sprint took place about four years ago, and *Bryony* sat in my computer as a nearly finished novel that just needed some poking for quite a long time.

It is very comforting for an author to have a nearly finished novel around. If your agent comes up to you and says "Have you got anything we can send them?" you can say "Funny you should ask…" If there is a hole in your self-imposed self-publishing schedule and that novella you were going to write went sideways on you, you can pull out your nearly finished novel and suddenly you are golden.

I am a little sad to lose this one to publication. I very much hope you enjoyed reading it, but now I no longer have the security of knowing that I can call on Bryony and her Beast in case of emergency.

Oh, well. It's a weird job, and nobody does it alone.

To my proofreaders, who will see this before anyone else— *thank you.*

Particular thanks to Cassie Dail who has read it more times than I care to contemplate because she had to read it once when I was panicking that it was too much like *Rose Daughter* which inspired it, and then once again looking for typos and for all I know, another time after I write these words because something will probably have gone wrong somewhere. Also, she came up with the title.

To my editor Brooke, who made me take out about sixty percent of the dashes and who is, as always, practical, invaluable, and snarky. (Wait, was I supposed to use a semicolon there? Brooke…!) She took the nearly-finished novel and filed off the "nearly" part.

To my friend MCA Hogarth (you should buy her books) who says smart things about self-publishing and draws honey badgers with me. Sometimes you need that.

To my readers, who actually buy these books, thank you! You are the reason I keep writing them. No, literally. If people didn't buy them, I would have to get a job and I am unfit for most forms of employment. I am very grateful.

And finally, to my husband, who reads the manuscripts and tells me if I am on the right track and also recently acquired a tiny tortoiseshell kitten who is making it really difficult to type this acknowledgments page. I love you very much, but about your cat…!

ABOUT THE AUTHOR

T. Kingfisher is a pen-name for the Hugo-Award winning author and illustrator Ursula Vernon.

Ms. Kingfisher lives in North Carolina with her husband, garden, and disobedient pets. Using Scrivener only for e-books, she chisels the bulk of her drafts into the walls of North Carolina's ancient & plentiful ziggurats. She is fond of wombats and sushi, but not in the same way.

You can find links to all these books, new releases, artwork, rambling blog posts, links to podcasts and more information about the author at

www.tkingfisher.com

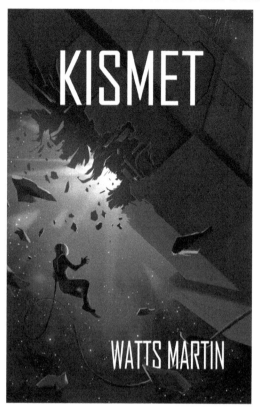

Tim Susman

THE TOWER and THE FOX

For Kip, growing up in shadow of the human men-only Prince George's College of Sorcery has been nineteen years of frustration. Magic comes naturally to him, yet he's not allowed to study sorcery because he's a Calatian—one of a magically created race of animal people. But when a mysterious attack leaves the masters desperate for apprentices, they throw their doors open, giving Kip his chance.

As he fights to prove his worth to the human sorcerers, he encounters other oddities: a voice that speaks only to him, a book that makes people forget he's there, and one of the masters who will only speak to him through a raven. Greater than any of those mysteries or even whether the College's attacker will return to finish the job is the mystery of how Kip and his friends can prove that this place is where they belong...

THE TOWER AND THE FOX BY TIM SUSMAN, $17.95 ISBN 978-1-61450-385-9

When Gerta's friend Kay is stolen away by the mysterious Snow Queen, it's up to Gerta to find him. Her journey will take her through a dangerous land of snow and witchcraft, accompanied only by a bandit and a talking raven. Can she win her friend's release, or will following her heart take her to unexpected places? A strange, sly retelling of Hans Christian Andersen's "Snow Queen," by T. Kingfisher, author of "Bryony and Roses" and "The Seventh Bride."

THE RAVEN AND THE REINDEER BY T. KINGFISHER, $12.95

ISBN 978-1-61450-389-7

Winner of the Nebula and WSFA Short Fiction Awards. Includes "The Tomato Thief" winner of 2017 Hugo Award - Best Novelette From award-winning author T. Kingfisher comes a collection of short stories, including "Jackalope Wives," "The Tomato Thief," "Pocosin," and many others. By turns funny, lyrical, angry and beautiful, this anthology includes two all-new stories, "Origin Story" and "Let Pass The Horses Black," appearing for the first time in print.

JACKALOPE WIVES AND OTHER STORIES BY T. KINGFISHER, $12.95

ISBN 978-1-61450-394-1

Printed in the USA
CPSIA information can be obtained
at www.ICGtesting.com
LVHW010920180824
788604LV00007B/129